CLAIMED BY PLEASURE

Also by Jaymie Holland

Taken by Passion

CLAIMED BY PLEASURE

JAYMIE HOLLAND

St. Martin's Griffin
New York

This is a work of fiction. All of the characters, organizations, and events portrayed in this novel are either products of the author's imagination or are used fictitiously.

www.stmartins.com

Book design by Anna Gorovoy

Library of Congress Cataloging-in-Publication Data

Holland, Jaymie.
    Claimed by pleasure / Jaymie Holland. — 1st ed.
        p. cm.
    ISBN 978-0-312-38667-2 (pbk.)
    1. Twins—Fiction.   2. Sisters—Fiction.   3. Missing persons—
Fiction.   4. Abduction—Fiction.   5. Shapeshifting—Fiction.
6. Supernatural—Fiction.   I. Title.
    PS3613.C38634C58 2011
    813'.6—dc23

                                                            2011026119

First published in the United States in e-book format under the title Wonderland: *King of Spades* by Ellora's Cave Publishing, Inc.

First St. Martin's Griffin Edition: November 2011

10   9   8   7   6   5   4   3   2   1

AUTHOR'S NOTE

DEAR READER,

The Wonderland series is back! *Claimed by Pleasure* is the second book in the four-book erotica series originally published with an e-publisher as Wonderland: *King of Spades* by Cheyenne McCray. It is published in its entirety.

This award-winning, bestselling romantic erotica Wonderland series is being republished under the name Jaymie Holland to clearly distinguish it from other works by me. I believe it is important that my readers know that when they read this series it is extreme in nature compared to other books by me they may have read before.

Claimed by Pleasure, as Wonderland: *King of Spades,* won the Golden Quill Award for Best Erotic Romance and was given rave reviews, including a four-star review from *RT Book Reviews.*

Author's note

I hope you enjoy *Claimed by Pleasure* and enjoy your journey through the door of a new discovery.

Cheyenne McCray
aka Jaymie Holland

CLAIMED BY PLEASURE

PROLOGUE

USING HIS MAGIC, KING DARRONN SHOVED open the doors and strode onto the private balcony of his château, his boot steps heavy thuds against the granite flooring. With a scowl he flexed his massive chest beneath his leather tunic, then braced his hands on the low balcony wall while he viewed his realm nestled in the great Tarok Mountains.

Smoke wisped from cabin chimneys in the village, the acrid scent mingling with damp forest smells of wet leaves, loam, and pine. Blue-green mist crept close to the ground and swirled around the feet of the villagers going about their daily duties. He leaned against the railing and watched a spotted *anlia* buck and his doe slip through the forest mist until he could no longer see the pair and could only scent them with his keen weretiger senses.

Ravenwood flowers perfumed the air from where they spilled down the wooden trellis from his balcony to the ground. The purple blooms fluttered in the wind and loose petals swirled away with the breeze.

A fierce growl rumbled within him, the sound lost in the thunder of the nearby falls. One day he might again experience pleasure at the sight of his splendid kingdom.

When I no longer fear for my subjects and their collective futures. When children once again scamper through the meadows and their voices ring over the hillsides.

Cool wind swept off the waterfall, over his face and bare arms, and lifted his long wood-brown hair away from his shoulders. The falls tumbled from the range's uppermost reaches to well below the Kingdom of Spades and the mountain village, and fed into the Tarok River. The invigorating wind cleared his senses and prepared him for the step he must now take for his people.

With the birth of werecub twins to the High King and Queen months ago, after a four-Tarok-month pregnancy, great joy spread throughout all of Tarok. When Queen Alice had conceived last spring, new hope had blossomed within the four kingdoms that Mikaela of Malachad's black reign of sorcery had come to an end. The hope had been that breaking her mindspells and bringing forth new life would allow all the women of Tarok to again be fertile.

Yet no other children had been conceived in the spring in any of the Tarok Kingdoms. And of course no other babes were born in the fall.

At the thought of his newborn niece and nephew, a surge of pride seized Darronn's chest and he gripped the railing tighter. The babes were healthy and growing quickly, as weretiger cubs should. The girl had been named Lexi, after the High Queen's sister who was somewhere on Earth, and the boy was Lancelot, a name Queen Alice fancied from her world. Odd names, both, but they suited the children who neared four Tarok months of age. The infants now crawled about and were into everything they could get their tiny hands on, much to the excitement of their mother, the consternation of their father, and the amusement of their three doting uncles.

On his last visit just a week ago, Darronn had clenched his jaw in frustration at the sight of the small army of guards his brother Jarronn was forced to keep around his infants and mate when he was not with them.

The cubs should only know the freedom of living in a Tarok Kingdom, he thought, *not cages of any kind.*

Over a long, brutal, and bloody summer, the four Kingdoms of Tarok had gone into battle with Mikaela's warriors and had dealt Malachad a devastating blow. Her warriors had retreated to lick their wounds, and the Kings of Tarok knew it was only a matter of time before they would go to battle once again. Now, months later, Mikaela had reasserted her menace. Her mind-powers were too great to discount and her *bakirs,* her legion of psychics, had regrouped and had recently begun mental attacks anew on the High King's court.

The bitch. Darronn bit back a snarl. Mikaela's betrayal of the Tarok clan had ripped at his soul, a jagged, poisonous wound that had eaten away at his heart since the moment he learned of her treachery. At one time he believed himself to be close to his younger sister, more so than his three brothers . . . but she had used him.

He tossed back his head and this time a savage roar ripped from his throat. The cry echoed throughout the mountainside kingdom. A cry of power and of the cunning he would use to aid Tarok in defeating the bitch . . . And a cry of powerlessness raging through his soul, because his people had gone nearly two decades with no conceptions, no births.

Mikaela sought revenge for being slighted when their parents split the larger Tarok Kingdom into four lesser kingdoms, and had bequeathed all to their four sons and nothing to their daughter. Before Mikaela had left to mate with King Balin of Malachad Kingdom, she had oft told Darronn he should be angered that his twin Jarronn had been made ruler over Tarok when he was but hours older than Darronn.

"*You* should be High King," she had said many times in the sweet voice she always used with him.

But he had simply responded, "Their choice was as it should be. Jarronn is far better suited to rule all of Tarok than I, and he is the eldest."

Darronn recalled the flicker of darkness in Mikaela's eyes. He should have known then, but his love for his younger sister had blinded him to her treachery.

"Master, it is time." Kalina's melodic voice floated over the roar of the waterfall, interrupting his dark thoughts.

With a frown, he turned to see the sorceress standing in the doorway to his chambers, her head bowed as she waited for his instruction. Having served the High King in the Kingdom of Hearts for over a decade, Kalina was well trained in her submissive role, and obviously relished it.

"Wait for me in my chambers," he commanded.

The sorceress bowed, and disappeared back through the doorway.

After one last look at his realm, Darronn strode across the balcony into his quarters, and closed the doors behind him. A fire burned in the hearth, taking the chill from the room. Kalina stood beside the glowing *a'bin*, the magical table she had transported with her when she recently joined him in the Kingdom of Spades.

Kalina's head remained bowed, her hands behind her back and her feet positioned well apart so that he might reach for her lusciousness beneath her scant black leather trappings. Unlike the Kingdom of Hearts, where most women wore almost nothing at all, Darronn preferred his women to wear leather. Kalina's dress had two thin straps crisscrossing her breasts and exposing her berry-dark nipples. Her belly and back were bare, but the bottom half covered her tiny ass and her bare mons. Still it was short enough to tease him with tantalizing views when she moved or bent over. Darronn's black and gold collar of ownership encircled her throat and from each of her recently pierced nipples swung a single gold spade charm.

Kalina wet her lips with her tongue, and he knew

that she wished for his cock. "What is your pleasure, Master?"

The room was warm from the fire burning in the hearth, vanquishing the chill from the balcony. At the sight of the lusty sorceress, a slight sheen of sweat coated Darronn's powerful body, his cock growing hard and erect. A feral purr rose up within him at the smell of Kalina's desire. He felt sorry for his brother Jarronn, who now only had one woman for his pleasure. However, Darronn did not at all mind the fact that as second born and heir-designate he inherited Kalina and would inherit anything else Jarronn released until Lance and Lexi were much older.

Darronn moved to the *a'bin*, where the sorceress stood, and turned his gaze to the three cards. It did not please him that he was forced to select his queen from a mere card, as his brother had. True, Jarronn's mate had been well chosen, and Darronn had certainly enjoyed mind-bonding with the High Queen.

Kalina's well-oiled body gleamed in the candlelight and she flicked her tongue along her red lips. "You must choose, Master."

"I did not ask your advice, wench." Darronn's muscles flexed as he caught Kalina's chin and forced the sorceress to look up at him. "Punishment is in order. Mayhap I should use my strap against your backside."

"If it pleases you, Master." Kalina's fire-ice eyes flared and the scent of her arousal grew stronger. "But first, you must choose."

Darronn's rumbling growl would have been enough to make any other of his subjects flinch, but not the sorceress. "Kneel," he commanded, and with a turn of his tattooed wrist he magically removed all his clothing so that he stood naked before her.

Kalina gracefully obeyed, lowering her eyes and holding her hands behind her back as she knelt.

Clenching one hand in her long black mane, Darronn tilted her head back so that her amber eyes met his. "Suck my cock while I choose my mate."

A sensual smile curved Kalina's lips. "Yes, Master."

Darronn pulled the sorceress to him by her hair and watched as his cock slid through her warm and anxious lips. For a few moments he thrust in and out as she flicked her tongue along his length, building the inferno of need within him that had never been fully quenched by any woman. The gold spades along her collar glittered in the candlelight and the gold baubles at her nipples swung faster with the intensity of her motions.

While Kalina sucked his cock, Darronn held his hand over the *a'bin,* and moved his palm above the three cards. At once the middle card glowed and a tiger emblem sparkled at its center. The rush of power that shot through Darronn bolted straight to his cock, making his erection tenser than ever, and Kalina moaned in excitement.

Without hesitating, Darronn scooped up the card and flipped it over in his palm, and he nearly climaxed from the desire that rushed through him.

Thick reddish-brown hair framed a beautiful face with lips made to kiss; full breasts created for him to suck; and long legs to slide between when he thrust his cock deep inside her. The woman's aqua eyes seemed familiar to him, much like Queen Alice's. But the woman's Tarok-sky gaze held fire and challenge, and Darronn knew she would not be easy to tame.

All the better. He tired of how easily wenches crawled into his bed. He craved a challenge, and he would have the redheaded woman begging for his cock even without his *tigri* pheromones.

With his magic he sent the card to his library for safekeeping, and then summoned his leather strap. The sorceress's eyes widened as the strap appeared.

"Raise your dress above your ass," he commanded as he trailed the strap over her bare back and arms.

The sorceress continued to suck his cock as she reached down and pulled her clothing up to her waist so that her ass was bared to him.

Darronn smiled. "This is for disobedience," he said as he swatted her backside with the black leather.

Kalina moaned around his cock, and he knew she reveled in both the sting and the thrill of his lash.

Darronn continued to lightly strap the sorceress while she pleasured him, leaving faint pink marks upon her pale flesh. His vision blurred as he imagined it was his future queen who sucked his cock, and his thrusts grew stronger. He would relish fucking the wench. He would enjoy turning her skin rosy with his strap, making it sting and tingle so much that she would beg him to drive into her harder and harder yet.

With a shout Darronn climaxed, followed by a roar, as he imagined his seed spilling into his future queen's womb.

CHAPTER ONE

WITH A SCOWL FIERCE ENOUGH TO SEND any guy in the bar diving for cover, Alexi O'Brien grabbed her bottled beer and chugged the contents. The icy, bitter fluid rolled down her throat, settling in a cold burn in her empty stomach. Hell, she ought to get a good buzz, and fast. She'd never been one for drinking, but today she needed something to dull the pain and anger she knew would never go away. Not unless—*until*—she found Alice.

Annie, their conservative cousin, frowned as Alexi slammed the bottle onto the rich mahogany bar and signaled the bartender for another round. Alexi cocked her head and studied her favorite cousin and best friend, Annie. Alexi knew that her cousin only needed her half-glasses for reading or painting. But, like Annie's plain-Jane clothing and her ever-present severe hairdo, the reading glasses were a way of hiding her true self from the world. If she'd just ditch the glasses, get a sexy wardrobe, and let her hair down, Annie would be absolutely stunning.

"Getting plastered isn't going to bring her back," Annie said in the soft southern accent she still had despite the fact she'd been living in San Francisco for over ten years. Although if she was pissed, that southern accent got hard in a hurry. She pushed her pewter-framed glasses up to the bridge of her nose then toyed with the straw in her sweet iced tea. "Alice wouldn't want you to be miserable, sugar. You know that."

Alexi raked her fingers through her wild auburn locks as the bartender placed another bottle in front of her. His appreciative gaze lingered on her slim form, trailing from her generous cleavage to the gold tiger charm dangling from the piercing at her belly button, and down to her tiny skirt.

"Don't drink those too fast," he said in a deep voice that made her nipples tighten against the flimsy material of her blouse. "You might do something you'll regret later, sweetheart."

"Oh, really?" Alexi studied him in a blatant perusal from his blue eyes on down. The guy was dark haired, muscular, and hot, as she usually liked her men, and she could almost imagine letting him tie her up while he slid into her. Would he be man enough? Damn, she hadn't thought about her bondage fantasy in a long while.

Her gaze slid over the bartender's snug black T-shirt to the hard-on pressing against his jeans as she thought of wild and wicked sex with him. Yeah, no doubt he'd give her a good ride. She bet he'd even enjoy participating in one of her favorite fantasies, the one where she was a French maid being erotically punished by her employer.

Alexi used to fuck 'em and leave 'em all the time because she didn't believe in long-term relationships or happily-ever-afters. But since Alice's disappearance, Alexi just didn't have it in her to flirt or have sex. The only reason she'd dressed this way tonight was because Annie had practically dared her, and Alexi never backed down from a challenge.

"If I get drunk enough, I might even find you attractive," she said to him with a sugar-sweet smile, and the bartender gave a good-natured grin. Alexi dismissed him with a little flick of her fingers and then crossed one leg over the other. Her skirt slid up, exposing a good inch of flesh above her thigh-high stockings.

Annie rolled her brown-sugar-colored eyes. "I can't believe you let that one go."

But this past year, Alexi always let them go. She couldn't enjoy herself without knowing that Alice was okay.

"Why did she vanish the way she did?" Alexi rubbed one of her gold bracelets, a habit she'd taken up when her twin disappeared—Alice used to rub her own bracelet all the time. "One year ago today. A *year*, Annie. I just can't believe it."

"You've got to get on with your life." With her index finger, Annie pushed her glasses back up her nose.

"You've done everything from mounting a well-publicized missing-persons campaign to hiring every private investigator in the city. You've almost exhausted your resources, your law practice is suffering . . . pretty soon you won't be able to afford to eat, much less search for Alice."

With a slow shake of her head, Alexi fixed her gaze on the beer bottle and picked at the label as that familiar sadness settled all around her like piles of legal briefs. "No real clues. Alice's purse and jacket scattered on the park bench . . . even her shoes left in the grass."

Alexi's brows narrowed as she remembered that day so clearly. While driving to the park on her Harley, moments after talking to Alice on her cell phone, Alexi had just *known* something had gone wrong. The link she'd had with her twin since birth had been severed as cleanly as if it had never existed. It was like there was a hole now where her sister should be . . . like a paper doll that had been cut out of a book and lost.

Alexi had arrived at the park, frantic, only to find no signs of Alice other than the items she'd left behind.

Sighing, Alexi tore a piece of label off her beer bottle, her twin gold bracelets glittering from her wrists with every movement she made. Moisture beaded on the bottle's brown surface, wetting her fingertips as she worked to strip the bottle bare.

A fresh wave of anger flushed over her at the memory of why Alice had gone to the park in the first place. She'd walked in on her cheating bastard ex-fiancé and caught him screwing their landlady while being taken in the ass by a guy in leather and chains. Alexi had

Maced the hell out of the three of them, but Alice had fled.

After Alexi had kicked the trio out of the apartment, she'd called Alice on her cell phone several times, but her twin had refused to come home, insisting that she needed to get away. Alice had mentioned the reason she'd been home early to begin with—her boss had fired her for refusing to suck his cock as part of her secretarial duties.

In the weeks following Alice's disappearance, Alexi had taken her fury out on the bastard and made him pay. She'd done her homework, and the accountant had gone down in a hurry for tax evasion.

Alexi took a couple more swallows of her beer before she thunked the bottle back onto the bar. "I'm going to find her, Annie. I know that she's out there somewhere. She's *not dead*, she's just missing."

Annie sipped her iced tea through the straw and carefully set it back on the drink coaster so that it was perfectly in the center. "You and the police have done everything you can."

But Alexi's mind slipped back in time, to the moment she'd parked the Hog, thrown her helmet aside, and run for the park bench. "Why did Alice stuff her bra and panties into her purse?" she mused aloud for the thousandth time. "If she'd been kidnapped and raped, it's not likely the person would have taken the time to leave Alice's underwear behind, so neatly tucked away."

As she frowned at her beer bottle, Alexi's head began to spin—from both the beer she'd chugged and the memories of Alice's disappearance. "Her bare footprints led around a tree . . . and then nothing. *Nothing*. It was like she'd been swallowed up whole."

Alexi turned her gaze to Annie who looked totally miserable now. "This was supposed to be a night to get your mind off everything for a little while," Annie said quietly. "Maybe this wasn't such a good idea."

"I'm sorry, honey." Alexi leaned over and hugged her cousin. Annie was soft and warm, and smelled of brown sugar and vanilla. When Alexi pulled away, she gave Annie the start of a smile. "You're right. I need to enjoy our time together and that's that."

The alcohol buzz hit Alexi hard. One minute she was feeling a little loose and the next she was good and tipsy. She was such a freaking lightweight, and a giggly drunk the rare times she reached that point. Alcohol made her real horny, too, but she wasn't likely to do anything about that, other than use one of her assorted vibrators when she got home.

She braced one elbow on the bar and trailed the fingers of her other hand over her sexy midriff top with the beaded fringe, down to the black miniskirt, and then pointed to the lipstick-red heels she'd put on at Annie's suggestion for their night out. "Maybe I ought to see if I can find a man and put this outfit and these 'fuck-me' shoes to good use. It's been over a year since I've had a good lay. I don't do celibacy well."

Annie rolled her eyes and Alexi had to grin. Her cousin lived alone with her cat, Abracadabra, and was an artist as well as a brilliant English lit professor. Annie looked the part, too, with her butt-length nut-brown hair pinned into a knot at her nape, and her ever-present loose skirts and blouses. Tonight Annie's version of a going-out-on-the-town dress was a simple black blouse and skirt that complemented her generous figure, but couldn't be called sexy in the slightest. And for all Alexi knew, Annie was still a virgin, 'cause she always got embarrassed when the subject of sex was brought up.

So Alexi almost fell off her barstool when Annie said, "I think you should. That is, er, get laid."

"Excuse me." Alexi held up one finger as she grabbed her beer with her free hand and chugged the rest of the bottle's contents. She banged the empty on the bar then turned back to her cousin. "Did you actually say the term 'get laid,' as in 'get fucked'?"

A deep rose flush stole over Annie's face. "Just because I'm not getting any, doesn't mean you shouldn't."

"Hmmmm." Alexi placed her finger on the tip of her nose and swayed as she eyed her cousin from head to toe. "I think this calls for a plan of action. A plan to get Annie laid."

"Um, no." The room's soft lighting reflected off of Annie's glasses as she retrieved her wallet from a pocket of her skirt. She pulled out enough to cover the tab and a tip. "I don't do casual sex."

This time Alexi snorted. "You don't do sex at all."

The color in Annie's cheeks flashed stoplight red and her voice rose an octave. "Ready for dinner? I made reservations at the seafood place next door."

Alexi's head spun from all the beer as she grabbed her jacket and purse, and slipped the long skinny strap of her purse onto her shoulder. "So that was your plan." She giggled and slid off the barstool, her tiny skirt riding up to her hips and flashing her bare ass cheeks and the strip of thong beneath. She didn't give a damn if anyone saw her butt—right now she was feeling fiiiiine. "You know I can't hold my alcohol. Figured you'd get me drunk and relaxed before dinner, did ya?"

Annie gripped Alexi's upper arm to steady her. "Worked, didn't it?" Annie glanced over Alexi's shoulder and muttered, "But I'd better get you out of here quick, before the big guy in all that black leather makes it over here."

"But I like men in black." Alexi tottered as Annie dragged her toward the bar's swinging doors. "I really like to get down and dirty with 'em. The tall, dark, and dangerous type. Maybe I'd even let him tie me up—if he's man enough to take me."

"Trust me, sweetheart." Annie gripped Alexi's arm tighter. "You don't want to mess with *that* one. Big. Hairy. And butt-ugly."

"Oh, Annie." Alexi giggled again and slipped her arm around her cousin's waist. "It's nice to have someone looking after *me* for a change."

It was midnight by the time the taxi pulled up to Alexi's pastel pink town house. She and Annie had enjoyed a relaxing evening of several courses, from shrimp cocktail to clam chowder, to Caesar salad, then grilled salmon, cheesecake for dessert, and coffee with Baileys afterward. Alexi had enjoyed a couple of glasses of wine during dinner, and had managed to keep up her good buzz, but she'd had to have her coffee afterward. If she didn't get her daily dose of caffeine, things could get ugly.

For a fraction of a second when she looked up at the dark town house, a sense of loneliness bled through Alexi and she wished she wouldn't be alone for at least one night. But she shoved the loneliness away, gave Annie a quick hug good-bye, and climbed out of the cab.

"Get some rest, y'hear?" Annie said as Alexi stood outside the car's door. "Need me to walk you to the door?"

"Okay and nope, I'm fine." Alexi gave her cousin a smile and tried not to wobble on her heels so Annie wouldn't realize just how tipsy she still was. "You made this night *so* much easier to get through."

Annie pushed her glasses up her nose and returned Alexi's smile. "For both of us."

After she shut the car's door, Alexi watched the taxi pull away until its red taillights disappeared over the hill.

With a sigh she turned, her purse slapping against her hip beneath her jacket. She tottered up the steps to the town house she'd been renting since Alice disappeared. It was supposed to have been a surprise for Alice—one of the partners at the firm where Alexi worked had taken a position in New York City. He'd agreed to rent the two-story town house to them at a rock-bottom rate. The day that Alice vanished, Alexi had finalized the deal.

The first week after Alice's disappearance, while she searched for her twin, Alexi had hired movers to bring all of Alice's belongings from that little apartment she'd lived in with her asshole ex-fiancé. Everything had been moved in and was ready for Alice, for the day when Alexi found her sister.

But she never did.

Shoving back the painful memories, Alexi reached the small concrete landing and grasped the old-fashioned brass door handle and paused. She almost didn't want to go into the house . . . to be alone again. She breathed deeply of the smells of ocean and fresh cut grass and allowed herself to enjoy the cool wind lifting her hair from around her face. A foghorn floated through the night along with the clanging sound of a ferry's bell.

After unlocking the door, she let herself into the dim interior lit only by a colorful stained-glass lamp on a small table in the foyer. One of Annie's beautiful seascape oil paintings graced the wall just above the table. Alexi locked the door behind her, then started to slip her jacket from her shoulders. Familiar odors of cinnamon potpourri and lemon furniture polish surrounded her, and she almost imagined she could smell the rose-scented lotion Alice used to use.

But then Alexi caught smells that didn't belong, and she dropped her jacket to the carpeted floor in a rush, freeing her arms. The unfamiliar scents set her senses on alert because they didn't belong in her home . . .

wildflowers, sunshine, and a fresh mountain breeze. Pleasant, yes, but they shouldn't have been there.

Her purse still hung from her shoulder, and she slipped her hand inside until her fingers met the cool Mace canister. Hair prickled at her nape while she withdrew the canister. Slowly she let her purse slide to the carpeted floor where it landed with a soft thud. Her heart pounded, and the pleasant buzz she'd had vanished.

An eerie blue glow flared from the direction of Alexi's bedroom.

Anger burned in her gut. Someone was in her home and she was going to kick the person's ass. She might not know tai chi like her aunt Awai, but Alexi worked out, she had Mace, and she had a hell of a temper that more than made up for her lack of martial arts training.

Mace held high in her left hand, Alexi gritted her teeth and silently eased down the plush carpeted steps and through the living room. She clenched her right hand into a fist, prepared to deck the son of a bitch once she nailed him with the Mace.

All her senses were on high alert, and her ankles didn't even wobble in the killer heels. When she reached the bedroom door she waited a second, then peeked around the door frame.

A giant mirror stood where her bed should be. An incredibly beautiful mirror with an ornate frame that glittered in the strange blue glow now filling her bedroom. Sparkles flashed within the blue misty glow, looking as though Tinkerbell had come for a visit.

What the hell?

Anger and confusion mingled with curiosity as Alexi moved toward the mirror. The bead fringe along her blouse caressed her belly as a breeze seemed to come from *inside* the mirror and flow out into the bedroom. Her steps faltered and she wondered if maybe she'd gotten a whole lot more buzzed than she'd originally thought. She had to be hallucinating—all of this.

When she finally reached the mirror she stood face-to-face with her reflection. Her almond-shaped turquoise eyes, her auburn hair, her hand held high, still gripping the Mace. What was she going to do, Mace her mirror image?

The whole moment was bizarre and surreal, and Alexi was sure she'd lost her grip on reality. Hell, maybe her sanity, too. She let the canister slip from her fingers and it gave a soft thump as it landed on the carpet. The gold bracelet on her wrist glittered in the room's eerie light as she raised her hand and placed her palm flat against the mirror's surface. It was smooth, but surprisingly warm to her touch.

It sure didn't feel like a hallucination.

Her reflection rippled and changed and Alexi's knees almost gave out.

A mountain meadow appeared, surrounded with thick forest to the left, a ridge of mountains to the right, and lots of wildflowers scattered through thick grass. A cool breeze washed over Alexi, fluttering the bead fringe at her belly and chilling the gold tiger charm at her navel. In the distance water tumbled down a steep mountainside and she heard the rumble of the falls and birds twittering. Rich scents swept over her with the breeze . . . smells of pine, damp forest loam, wildflowers, and fresh water.

Okay, she was certifiable. Call the funny farm, because Alexi O'Brien had done lost it. No more beer for her—crappy-tasting stuff, anyway. She might as well just curl up on the floor, take a nap, and sleep it off.

A man moved into her mirror view, and Alexi thought she was going to scream.

That or orgasm, because he was the most gorgeous, most dangerous-looking man she'd ever seen . . . and his penetrating green eyes were staring right at her, as if he could *see* her.

Alexi's nipples tightened beneath her scanty midriff top. *Damn,* this was one fine hallucination.

The man held up a golden playing card and the muscles of his bare chest and arms rippled with power. His features were strong and chiseled and his long wood-brown hair stirred around his shoulders in the breeze. He looked bad to the bone from the gold earring he sported in his left ear to the tattoo of a spade on his left wrist, to—*hold on*—to that one hell of a package between his powerful black-clad thighs. She'd bet he'd be man enough to take her on. Maybe even man enough to tie her up and give her one hell of a ride.

Alexi sucked in her breath and pressed her palm tighter to the mirror. *Damn. If he were real I'd fuck him in a heartbeat.*

The hallucination man's lips quirked and Alexi

23

thought she'd climax just from the sinfully sensual movement.

Time to get out the vibrator.

With a twist of his fingers, the golden card vanished. On his side of the mirror, he raised his hand and placed his palm against Alexi's.

Shock tore through her at the feel of his warm, callused hand against her palm. When his fingers interlocked with hers, Alexi gasped and tried to free herself, but he was too powerful.

The man pulled, and she stared in horrified fascination as her hand and wrist slipped *into* the mirror. It felt like she was being drawn through a Jell-O wall.

She struggled for real then, fighting to get away from his grip. "Let me go, you son of a bitch!"

A predatory rumble rose up from the man and he yanked her arm. Alexi screamed and pitched forward, right through the mirror.

CHAPTER TWO

THE WOMAN WAS A FIGHTER, AND DARRONN'S cock stiffened in appreciation of her fiery spirit. Even as he drew her toward him through the looking glass, the woman struggled. Her nipples poked against the flimsy material of her clothing and he scented her feminine heat, the desire that had flooded her while she had stared at him through the sorceress's magical looking glass.

Fear and fury blazed in her aqua eyes as he pulled her through and she shouted, "Let me go, you son of a bitch!"

Lust raged through Darronn and he tired of waiting for his mate. With little effort, he tugged, and the woman screamed as he brought her into his arms.

"Bastard!" she shouted as she slammed her right fist into his eye and rammed her knee into his groin.

Searing pain in his cock and bollocks drove Darronn to his knees . . . pain unlike any he had felt in his over two hundred Tarok years. White sparks burst in his head, fire burned through his groin, and fury flamed in his gut.

How dare the wench strike the King of Spades!

The woman whirled toward the looking glass and started to step through it. With a roar, Darronn shifted into his white tiger form and tackled her, knocking her sideways. He roughly pinned her shoulders to the grass with his massive paws, and had her flat on her back. Without putting all his weight on the woman, which would crush her, he settled between her thighs so that her entire body was immobile. He wasn't about to let her kick his bollocks again, regardless of what form he was in.

"Oh, shit," the woman whispered as she stared up at him, the smell of her fear and the throbbing pulse at her throat affirming her terror. "Nice kitty?"

Darronn roared with all the power of his species, and the woman's face turned as white as a snowburst bloom. Fear was a good place to start teaching the wench a lesson.

Alexi stared up at the tiger pinning her to the ground, and her mind hurtled through all her options. She was going to die. No . . . no, she wouldn't accept death. There had to be a way to keep the beast from eating her.

Adrenaline pumped through her body, causing every inch of her to tremble. Her back ached from landing so hard on the ground and her knuckles throbbed from that punch to the guy's eye. She dared to glance away from the tiger to where she'd decked the man—but he wasn't there. Although the bastard didn't seem the type to leave a woman to be a meal for a huge tiger, he must have fled when the beast jumped her.

But wait, this couldn't be real. *Get serious, Alexi.* Falling through a mirror and now trapped beneath a giant white tiger . . . This was nuts. She was just having one hell of a nightmare.

Her eyes met the intense green stare of the gigantic cat and chills rolled down her spine. No dream or nightmare had ever been this real, this vivid, this intense. Pebbles poked at her backside and grass tickled the exposed flesh on her arms, the base of her neck, and her ass, since the tiny skirt was now riding up around her waist. Wind blew through the meadow, ruffling the tiger's glossy white coat and rustling the surrounding trees. The beast's fur was soft against her bare belly and her hips—which didn't make sense if he was a wild animal.

"Are you someone's pet?" Alexi asked, as if the tiger could respond. "You haven't, er, eaten me yet."

The beast narrowed his gaze. *I always play with my food before I dine,* came a low and powerful voice in Alexi's mind, and she almost wet her panties.

"Some jerk must have slipped something into my drink." Alexi closed her eyes, forcing away the all too real image, and tried to calm the frantic racing of her heart. "That's the only explanation. I've been drugged and I'm just going to have to ride this out." She paused and swallowed. "And then I'll hunt down the bastard who did it and sue his sorry ass. Right after I kill him."

A rumble that sounded more like a chuckle rose up from the tiger hallucination that she could no longer see because she'd closed her eyes. Most unlike the way the rational and kickass Alexi handled problems, the drunk and drugged Alexi decided there was no way to fight a hallucination, so she might as well pretend none of this was happening, and the tiger didn't exist.

The beast's imaginary musk was strong, its weight still pressed against her. The hallucination shifted its bulk and Alexi felt a muzzle between her breasts, the light scrape of teeth, and then heard the distinct sound of cloth ripping. A tug at the flimsy clasp of her bra, and then the rush of cool air over her breasts. Her nipples tightened to hard peaks that made her squirm.

Okay, this hallucination feels far too real. I've seriously gone over the edge.

A rough tongue laved one nipple, sending a thrill straight through her and hardening her nipples even more.

Alexi's eyes popped open. The tiger lifted its giant head, and if she didn't know better, she'd swear the beast was pleased with her body's response.

The tiger hallucination sort of shimmered and started to change. To *shift*. White fur melted away to olive skin and wood-brown hair. Paws, forelegs, and tiger body changed to a naked muscled chest . . . and suddenly it was the gorgeous man who had yanked her through the imaginary mirror.

Giving in to the assurance that she'd totally lost all semblance of her sanity, Alexi stared up at the gorgeous face of the man she'd decked only moments before. The skin around his eye had already started to purple, and his furious expression told her he was none too pleased with her.

"You have already earned the severest of punishments." The man's voice vibrated through her, and sounded like the one she'd heard in her head when the tiger had her pinned. He had an unusual accent, maybe European. "You have much to learn, wench."

"Wench?" Hallucination or no, she wasn't taking that crap from anyone. Even if the timbre of his voice made her wet when he said the word. "My name is Alexi O'Brien—Ms. O'Brien to you, bastard. I have no intention of being punished by you or anyone else. I'm not a child, damn it."

With a scowl the man raised up just enough to work the torn blouse and bra the rest of the way from her torso. Fear and anger drove Alexi as she attempted to fight him, but he was too fast, too strong.

When she was naked from the waist up, he grabbed both her wrists with his hands, forcing them together so that her twin gold bracelets met. When he released her, she tried to pull them apart, but somehow the gold had been welded together, shackling her.

Alexi struggled against her bonds and tried to move her legs, which were still pinned beneath his weight. She gave him her fiercest glare and shouted, "Let me go, you prick."

The man's smile was both dangerous and sensual as he placed his palms over both her breasts and pinched her nipples. Alexi gasped and fought not to shrink away from his touch . . . or arch into it.

This is all too freaking weird.

"I am Darronn, Ruler of the Kingdom of Spades," he said as he continued to pinch and pull her nipples. "You will call me Master."

Anger burned through Alexi at his demand. "Fuck you!" She thrust her bound arms upward, planning to catch him on the chin, but this time he was ready for her.

The man who called himself Darronn caught her wrists, his huge hand dwarfing both of hers. He forced her arms up over her head and in one smooth move scooted up so that he straddled her, keeping her hips pinned as he responded, "Yes, I will fuck you. Many, many times. Many, many ways."

"I'll kill you before I'll let you rape me." Alexi struggled with everything she had, but it was like fighting against a granite statue. A statue that moved. A statue that had an enormous erection poking against his black pants.

A hard-on that part of her wanted to see, feel, touch, and taste.

Shit. She'd done lost it.

"You will beg me for my cock before I take you." The man kept her wrists pinned to the ground above her.

"Like hell—" she started, but then snapped her mouth shut when he held his free hand up and a black strap appeared in his grip, along with a three-foot-long golden stake.

How the hell did he do that? Alexi's skin chilled. And never mind the strap. What was he going to do with that stake?

In a quick movement he reached above her and buried the gold stake in the ground. Before she could comprehend exactly what he was doing, he'd tied her bound hands to the stake with the black strap. Her hands gripped the cool metal between her palms—as cold as the jolt of fear that shot through her body.

Yet somehow, unbelievably, the chill of fear was chased away by searing lust. Her earlier thoughts came back to her—she had finally met the man it would take to tie her up . . . and maybe even screw her like she'd often fantasized about.

What was she, crazy? Fantasy was one thing, but the reality . . . was both frightening and arousing all at once.

Darronn leaned back on his haunches and enjoyed the pleasing view of his future queen with her arms high over her head and bound to the stake. Rage burned in her aqua eyes. The fire and spirit in her gaze pleased him, and he looked forward to the challenge of taming her. No doubt she would enjoy rough sexual play as much as he did, and when the time came he would relish bringing her to their mutual pleasure.

But first, he had to help her understand what she truly wanted, to help her free herself from the confines she had so long been accustomed to accepting. Indeed, there was no man in her pathetic dimension worthy of her. No wonder she felt as if she must master the world, single-handedly.

With him, she would find the care and support she needed as deeply as her own breath. If she didn't poke out his eyes and sever his bollocks first.

He moved his gaze to her full, sensuous lips, imagined the feel of her mouth sliding over his cock and gave a rumbling purr.

"Let me go, damn you," the woman called Alexi demanded.

She had ordered him to call her Miz-o-brien in a tone that told him the name was reserved for those subservient to her. He could easily imagine her a queen of the realm from whence she came. Once she learned her place, she would serve well at his side.

The ache in his cock grew fiercer as his gaze lingered on her breasts, now exposed to Tarok's aging winter sun. In days it would be spring, as evidenced by the blooms scattered over his mountain, and the soft new grass beneath his mate's back.

Her reddish-brown hair fluttered in the chill wind to either side of her face. Gooseflesh pebbled her fair skin and plumped her ripe nipples. "Such riches," he murmured as he took them in hand at once. He would enjoy piercing her nipples and placing his signs of ownership upon her.

When he pinched her taut nubs between his thumb and forefinger, Alexi gasped, then visibly tensed her jaw as if trying to hold back a moan. Darronn's purr of satisfaction rumbled through his chest again. Yes, the wench enjoyed his touch, no matter that she would deny it should he give mention of the fact.

The furious look returned to her eyes. "Get off me, you sorry son of a bitch."

Darronn merely studied her while he used his magic to retrieve two more golden stakes and two black straps from his château. Her eyes widened and she attempted to struggle against her wrist bonds and to move her legs from beneath him.

Of course, his strength was too superior, and by simply placing part of his weight on one leg, he kept the other motionless with one hand while driving one stake into the ground with his other. He strapped her free ankle to it, forcing her legs apart.

In moments he had both of her legs bound and she was splayed wide for him. Except that he couldn't see all her delectable flesh, due to a strip of cloth covering her mound and folds. Her musk had been driving him wild with need since the first whiff he had caught through the looking glass.

"Damn you." Alexi struggled against her bonds one last time and then gave up, for the moment. Already she was exhausted, and it wouldn't do her a damn bit of good to fight right now. She needed to conserve her strength, and then when she had the opportunity she'd escape. After she killed the bastard.

When had she realized that this wasn't a hallucination or a dream? Somewhere along the line, her black-and-white brain had told her that too many things about the experience indicated that this was reality. She wasn't prone to a high level of imagination, and there weren't many gray areas in her past experience. It either was or it wasn't, and all her instincts told her this *was* real. Even the shapeshifting thing—going from tiger to man.

Shit. I am nuts.

And she was now very aware of how exposed she was to his gaze. Her blouse and bra torn away, her skirt up over her hips, her legs splayed wide and bound to stakes, and only her thong covering her—and not very well at that. It rode up between her folds and the crack of her ass.

Just because her body responded to his touch, and the struggle had turned her on, it didn't mean that she wanted him. And if she kept telling herself that, she might even believe it.

Damn.

"You no longer need this," the man said as he knelt between her splayed thighs and reached for her skirt. As if it was made of paper, he tore the flimsy black material, pulled it away from her body, and tossed it aside.

Alexi stared up at the beast of a man. Hunger raged in his eyes, and despite her position and being at this stranger's mercy, her body responded to him.

She had to gain some kind of control. Maybe make him see reason. "Why are you doing this?"

"You belong to me." He lowered his nose and sniffed at the black thong covering her mound. "I claim only what is my own."

Alexi gasped at the sensuality of what he'd just done. She fought against her body's reaction and shook her head, grass tickling her cheeks with the movement. "Like hell I belong to you, you kidnapping, raping asshole."

Darronn nuzzled her mound and she bit back a moan. She realized that a part of her wanted to give in to the sensations. Wanted to be tied up and taken. By *him*.

This was insane. She shouldn't want this man who had abducted her out of her home and now had her spread out like a gourmet dinner.

With his teeth he grasped the slender side strap of her thong and tore it apart. Alexi had no choice but to watch as he ripped away the other side as well. Her clit throbbed and her breasts ached. It had been so long since she'd had a man's cock inside her, felt the weight of him against her as he slid into her.

And she'd never had a man like this one.

Darronn turned her on more than she wanted to admit. He was all man, from the ripple of muscles in his body, to the power in his sensuous movements, to the heat in his gaze. Yeah, she'd fantasized about being tied up, leading to a long bout of wild sex, but Alexi had never thought she could give up enough control to let that happen—until now. Which was absolutely bizarre considering her circumstances.

Darronn grasped the loose cloth of her thong in his teeth and tugged. It slipped away, leaving her quim completely open to him.

Resting on his haunches, he brought the woman's cloth to his nose. He inhaled her scent from the damp material, imprinting Alexi's smell upon his senses and causing his cock to expand near to bursting for her. He tossed the cloth onto the grass and returned his gaze to hers.

Her glare was defiant, but her pupils dilated, her skin flushed with arousal, her mons glistening with her need for his cock. The urge to take her now was almost more than he could control, but he would not. Not until her need for him was so great that she begged for his cock in her quim. When she made the free choice to take him, then and only then would he sink his cock inside her core.

Despite what she might think, he was no rapist. He would never give a woman more—or less—than she wanted. Most especially his newfound mate.

The wench was now naked save for the black silk encasing each of her legs from thigh to toe, and the odd red slippers with sticks at the heels covering her feet. Darronn slowly slid his hand down the silken material on one of her legs and rumbled his approval. "I wish for you to wear these, and only these, in my presence."

"Bastard." A lesser man would surely burst into flame from the blaze in her eyes as she once again spat the word questioning his parentage.

Darronn lowered himself between her thighs, bracing his weight on his arms so that he remained above her. Alexi's throat worked and her expression shifted from fury to desire and back. "The sooner you realize you are my possession, the sooner you will learn what it is to be pleasured by the King of Spades."

"You're delusional, you know that?" Alexi snapped, only feeling like *she* was the delusional one.

His long brown hair drifted over her shoulder as he

nuzzled her throat, and Alexi fought to hold back a moan from the sensual feel of his stubbled cheeks chafing her neck, and the caress of his hair over her skin. "You smell as sweet as starflowers and midnight beneath the falls."

Now where did such a barbarian learn romantic talk like that?

"Stop touching me," she said in her best courtroom attorney voice, but to no surprise he ignored her.

Alexi expected to feel the weight of his body against hers—craved it, even—but his powerful arms kept him braced above her. This was a man who took what he wanted, and didn't hold back. So why was he holding back with her?

She closed her eyes, blocking out the sight of his handsome face as he moved his mouth down between the valley of her breasts. His lips brushed her skin in whisper-soft movements as he trailed them over the curve of one breast to lightly skirt the nipple. What was wrong with her? She wanted to arch her back and force her nipple into his mouth. She wanted him to suck it with the force of his desire for her.

No, no, no!

Darronn released a rumbling purr as he eased down Alexi's body, teasing her, making her recognize how much she needed him. The wench wanted him so badly that she was quivering, but she held back her moans admirably well. When he reached the gold piercing at her navel, he smiled. A tiger bauble. Most suitable for his tigress, yes.

He flicked his tongue against the gold, then drove his tongue into her navel. Alexi gasped and the scent of her magnified. His purr grew louder.

"This is crazy." Her voice came in ragged huffs. "You can't just kidnap a person and tie them up. It's not right."

"But I did not kidnap you. I rescued you from a bleak exile and brought you to your rightful home." Darronn abandoned her navel for lower pursuits, softly nuzzling her belly and reaching the smooth skin of her shaved mound. His erection grew, threatening to spill his seed. A fine lot that would be, to climax in his breeches. "You are mine now, as it should be."

His tigress growled. "I don't belong to *anyone* but myself, dickhead."

Darronn's nose skimmed her swollen folds, and Alexi's thighs trembled on either side of his head. Likely she would climax with one flick of his tongue against her engorged clit. As much as he would enjoy giving her pleasure, he intended for her to want him with no regrets whatsoever, and under his terms.

Alexi was going to scream if she didn't come soon. The bastard was hardly touching her and she was *so* on the edge. She hated him, she wanted him. She wanted to kill him, she wanted him to screw her. Shit, she couldn't take much more of this.

Darronn moved away and she opened her eyes to see him standing between her splayed thighs. She expected him to kick off his boots, tear off his pants, and then drive his cock into her. But he merely studied her, his arms folded across his chest, the wind tossing his long hair. The bruise at his eye was darker now, and she only wished she'd blackened them both. Maybe then she would have had a chance to get back through that mirror.

That was what she wanted, wasn't it?

"You have come to a world you do not understand, my firecat, and you have met a man you cannot command," he said in his firm yet vibrant tone. "For your own good, you must learn the desires and fears of your heart—and you must learn to trust and respect the one person with the skill and power to make you whole." He paused and then added, "Me."

Alexi just stared at him, unable to believe he had the nerve to tell her she needed to be taught any lessons. "You're out of your mind, you know that?"

"It matters not if you believe me, or even if you refuse your own desires—not yet—so long as you learn obedience. We begin your training now, as there is no time to waste. Your punishment for striking a King of Tarok, and for your rudeness," he said, "will be to remain here the night through."

Alexi's jaw dropped and she stared at the bastard in utter disbelief. He was going to leave her staked out in the middle of a mountain meadow? Naked?

"With my protections you will remain safe here, and no harm shall come to you." He raised his hands and a red shimmer filled the air around Alexi, like a fiery bubble, and then it was gone. "When I return for you in the morning, you will address me as Master, and with respect, or I will not free you. Do you understand?"

39

"Screw you." Alexi clenched her teeth and her ears rang with the rage ripping through her.

Darronn gave a slow nod, his expression stern. "I see that you do understand," he said before he turned and walked away.

CHAPTER THREE

ALEXI LET LOOSE WITH A SCREAM OF FURY. With all the strength she had, she yanked against her bonds. The leather straps bit into her wrists and ankles and her muscles ached with the effort of her struggles.

The straps didn't budge. Not that she'd thought they would.

Shit shit shit. Calm down. This isn't going to get you out of here, Alexi O'Brien.

Forcing herself to relax her muscles, she slowly turned her head from one side to the other, and tried to tilt her head to look behind her as best she could. No sign of the bastard. Just trees, grass, mountains, flowers . . . yadda yadda yadda.

Alexi's breathing and her heart rate were surprisingly even and calm considering her circumstances. But she was incredibly turned on, and that pissed her off and excited her all at once. How could being abducted by a gorgeous Conan the Barbarian, and staked out like an offering to the gods, make her so hot?

But with her legs spread wide, she was more than wet, her folds swollen, and her clit throbbing. Her breasts jutted up, her nipples hard as gemstones, her arms stretched way overhead, and her hands still gripped the gold stake. She wished she could ride the smooth, round end of the stake right now to get some relief. Damn, but she needed to climax.

More than likely this was due to her year of celibacy. Annie was right—she shouldn't have so completely neglected herself. Then she wouldn't be so desperate to be fucked by her captor.

Even if he made her body vibrate with just one look.

He's a rapist, damn it. But her mind pushed back against the thought. She sensed plenty of aggression and power in tiger-man . . . but no malice. No intent to truly take her against her will, beyond what he had already done.

So, it'll be a battle of wills. So be it.

Alexi sighed and stared up at the strange blue-green clouds above her in the darkening sky. The clouds moved as though a gentle wind pushed them, but she couldn't feel a breeze or hear the waterfall. She felt surprisingly warm and comfortable, as though she was within a room, rather than outside in the middle of nowhere. Even the pebbles that had been poking into her back no longer bothered her, and it was like she was lying on a soft bed of velvet instead of grass. Weird.

Time to take stock and formulate a plan.

She was staked out and naked (thigh-highs and stilettos did *not* count as clothing), and entirely vulnerable to man or beast . . . or men who were both. She was in the middle of a meadow filled with trees, flowers, and bushes that didn't look like anything she'd ever seen before. Not that she'd ever been into nature—she was a city girl and a lawyer for crissake. What did she know about rural anything?

Good thing she'd peed before she left the restaurant. But what would she do if he wouldn't let her up later?

Her knuckles still throbbed from slamming her fist into the bastard's eye—Darronn, he'd said his name was. Although he'd insisted she call him Master. Asshole. She'd show him who was Master.

Obedience, my ass.

Even though she didn't give a damn what he'd said, his words echoed through her mind. *"You have come to a world you do not understand, my firecat, and you have met a man you cannot command."*

A world she didn't understand . . . he'd gotten that part right. She didn't understand how any of this could be real, or even how she knew it was. Was this a world full of men who tied up women who refused to call them Master? Great.

The part about not being able to command him, well, she could certainly see that—no man she'd ever known was like him, and damn him, but he turned her on more than she wanted to admit.

What he was going to find out, though, was that

he'd just met a woman whom *he* couldn't command. Yeah, they'd kill each other in no time.

She couldn't help but picture the sincerity in his eyes when he'd said, *"For your own good, you must learn the desires and fears of your heart . . ."*

As if there was anything that *he* could teach *her*. She always knew what she wanted, and when she found it, she went for it. She didn't need some tattooed, green-eyed, gorgeous Neanderthal to teach her anything.

As for fear, she feared nothing when it came to her heart. Long ago she'd learned her lesson, and she didn't let any man come close enough to hurt her. So what was there to fear?

". . . and you must learn to trust and respect the one person with the skill and power to make you whole. Me."

Oh, yeah, sure. *As if* she'd trust and respect a brute who'd yanked her through a mirror, turned into a tiger and tackled her, then left her staked out, alone, in the middle of nowhere. Hot and horny at that.

Bastard.

Damn, but it pissed her off to want him so badly when she should hate him. What was it about him? Something told her there was more to him than just an arrogant prick who liked to order women around. Despite his domineering manner, he'd seemed somehow sincere and caring.

Alexi rolled her eyes and sighed. Well, that made *lots* of sense. She was staked and bound and at her captor's complete mercy, and she thought he'd seemed caring. Once she got back to San Francisco, she'd have to visit a shrink for sure. Maybe Alice's disappearance had affected her more than she'd realized. She would just close her eyes, go to sleep, and hopefully wake up in her own bed.

Darronn shifted into a tiger and paced the edge of the Tarok Forest, his gaze focused on the maid staked out in the meadow. He would never leave Alexi, or any of his subjects, alone and vulnerable. He would stay with her as long as it took for her to learn what was necessary to heal her heart and soul.

He had no doubt that when she gave in to his wish, at first it would be merely as a way to be free of her bonds. But it would be a start, and she would soon learn to bow to all his demands.

Wind ruffled his fur as he quietly continued his pacing. She would be comfortable on the grass for the night as he had used his magic to place a black velvet cushion at her back. Air remained still within the protective bubble he had put around his future mate, and the temperature would remain constant and comfortable, so long as it surrounded her. Nights in the Kingdom of Spades were still cold through most of spring, but the dome would protect her, just as his fur protected him. She would not be able to smell, hear, or feel the world around her, beyond the barrier, but she would be safe.

The sun had reached the horizon, casting golden light over his mountain, and caressing the meadow with its last rays. Darronn's ears twitched, his sensitive hearing attuned to squirrels and *calin* scampering along the boughs of the *ch'tok* and *sini* trees.

In the distance a mountain wolf howled, one of Lord Kir's pack, and Darronn heard the sounds of many paws, hooves, and tiny feet of forest creatures scrambling for safety from the predator. The cave-dwelling wolves of Emerald City reigned over the lands on the other side of the mountain and beneath it, although they often traveled the Yellow Road between their realm and Tarok.

As he continued to pace, Darronn sensed the range of emotions sifting through Alexi—from anger to lust to frustration to calm consideration. Like his brothers, Darronn could not read minds, but he could sense emotions of those in his presence.

Unless the person knew how to hide their true emotions, a rare skill that Mikaela had perfected. Darronn rumbled and bared his teeth at the thought of his traitorous sister. He and his brothers had never sensed the blackness that had claimed her heart and soul. Even now a part of him ached to rescue the sister he had loved.

What would I give to erase the damage done by my parents' choice?

Or could Jarronn be right . . . that the blackness had already existed within Mikaela? Jarronn believed that the former High King and Queen had recognized this evil and made the choice they felt was best for all of Tarok. Darronn . . . wasn't so sure.

But then I was a fool, blindly trusting Mikaela until her betrayal.

Not only could she mask her true feelings, Mikaela had also been born with the gift of being able to read a person's thoughts if they were projected loudly enough. When they were young, in their twenties or so, the four brothers had all eventually learned to shield their minds from their sister. Until they had mastered the ability to block her, Mikaela had enjoyed mentally spying on the young men and teasing them with whatever she had learned. Whether it was mischief they had been into, or an early sexual escapade, she found out all she could about them. It had taken much schooling from the sorceress Leeani for the young men to master hiding their thoughts, and that had been well over two hundred years ago.

At the memory of the sorceress, a chuckling purr rose up within Darronn. How he and his brothers had lusted for their former teacher. The charms dangling from Leeani's dark nipples and her sensuous voice had been distracting to the young men. Surely it took them far longer to learn the lesson than they would have if their teacher had been one of the elder, decrepit sorcerers.

Darronn shook his massive head and raised his muzzle into the wind. Alexi's perfume of starflower and midnight still hung on the breeze. He scented an *anlia* buck nearby, too, and hunger burned in his belly for fresh meat. But he would not leave his woman for a moment, not even to assuage his thirst. If need be he could magically summon Kalina to watch her, but he chose to remain with his future queen.

He had sensed that Alexi felt no hunger, and had caught the scent of wine and good food on her warm breath. Fire burned in his loins, and the desire for his mate was near to overwhelming. Such a challenge she would be to tame . . . a challenge he would most certainly relish.

A warm mouth brushed over Alexi's, and she parted her lips and gave a soft moan. Firm lips pressed tight to hers, and stubble scraped her skin as a tongue darted inside. With a soft moan of surrender she invited the man's tongue deeper, invited him to fill her mouth in the same way she wanted his cock to fill her.

She could hear a waterfall pounding in the distance, birds chirruping, and the sound of wind through trees. Smells were keen, too. Grass and a wildflower perfume . . . and the drugging smell of a man.

His weight pressed against her, leather shirt and pants tight to her naked flesh. She ground her mound against his raging erection, needing this so badly, wanting it with everything she had.

Slowly Alexi's eyes opened and she saw Darronn above her with a smile so carnal that thrills ran straight from her nipples to that place between her thighs and back. His hips pressed tight to hers and his hands were braced to either side of her breasts. Surrounding his dark features, his wood-brown mane hung down long enough to tease her breasts.

She'd always thought a man with long hair was sexy, and damned if he wasn't that and more. His gold earring glinted in the morning sunlight, stubble roughened his jaw, and the bruise purpling the skin below his eye made him look even more rugged and dangerous than he had before.

This was real. *He* was real.

At that moment Alexi didn't know whether to rage at him for kidnapping her and tying her up . . . or to beg him to take her.

Always-in-control, decisive, man-eating Alexi O'Brien was at a loss for words for the first time in her adult life.

She was a sexual harassment lawyer, for crissake, and she went after those assholes with a vengeance. She *always* knew what to say, she *always* won her cases, and she didn't put up with shit from anyone. After what she'd gone through in law school, Alexi had done everything she could as a lawyer to prosecute every son of a bitch who thought he could get away with using his strength and position to intimidate her clients.

And her clients weren't always women. Several were men who either had a domineering woman trying to force them into bed by threatening their jobs, or a man who wanted to screw 'em in the ass. She had nothing against any kind of sex, as long as it was consensual, but if it wasn't, watch out, 'cause Alexi would nail the rapist's sorry carcass to the floor.

She'd gone after all of them with everything she

had, and had never lost a case. As if that would make up for the harassment she had experienced at the hands of her law school instructors.

But as she stared up at Darronn, it was as if all of her anger and her wounds had been stripped away, like her clothing, leaving only a woman. And this woman wanted this man more than anything. Right here. Right now.

It didn't make sense at all. None of it.

"My firecat wakes." Darronn lowered his head and brushed his lips over hers again. He smelled of forest breezes and a primal male musk that seeped into her blood like alcohol, intoxicating her just as much. "Do you desire me as badly as I desire you?" he asked.

"No." Alexi forced out the lie as she shifted against her bonds and tried not to moan from his sensual touches and words. She had to get her head back together. "And I'm not your anything."

A purr rumbled up from his chest, reminding Alexi that this man could turn into a real tiger. "You want my cock thrusting into your core," he said softly as his mouth moved to her ear. "I will fill you like no other man could. Or ever will again."

"You're deranged," Alexi replied, even as her body was on fire for him. Even as she arched up, pressing her breasts and mound tighter to his leather-clad muscles.

His stubble scraped her jaw as he moved his mouth back to hers. "Am I, wench?" He nipped at her lower lip, causing her to gasp from the pain and the thrill of it. "I think not."

Alexi wanted him so badly right now she didn't care

how he took her, just so long as he thrust his cock inside her, so hard and so fast that she could feel it all the way to her throat.

But first she needed to pee really, *really* bad.

"Untie me," she said with as much force as she could, although her demand sounded as empty as the feeling behind it. "I have to relieve myself."

For a moment he studied her then nodded. With a wave of his spade-tattooed wrist, her bonds were freed.

Alexi gave him a wary look as he helped her to her feet then gripped her upper arms for a moment. Her muscles ached from being bound for so long, and if he hadn't been holding her she probably would have fallen. She glanced down and saw that she had been lying on velvet. Somehow he'd managed to place a black velvet cushion beneath her.

"Listen, I've got to go really bad." Her gaze darted to the nearby trees and back to Darronn. "Just give me a moment alone, all right?"

He nodded and she headed toward the bush, her stilettos wobbling as she walked over the uneven ground through an odd blue-green morning mist. Her head ached from not having her morning coffee and her knuckles throbbed from punching the big horny gorilla last night.

Once she positioned herself behind the bush, she thought she'd pee forever, but it gave her time to think. It occurred to her that she could sneak away and hide out in the forest before he had a chance to catch her.

Alexi finished her business, stood, and started to

move into the forest, her heels wobbling as she walked over the rough ground. She'd have to take the damn things off, she thought as she rounded a tree—

And smacked right into Darronn.

"The meadow is in the other direction," he said as he caught her upper arms. "Did you forget so easily?"

Before she could answer, he grabbed her around the waist and flung her over his shoulder.

Alexi screamed and pounded her fists on his rock-hard ass. "Let me go!"

But the man was amazingly fast. Next thing she knew she was lying on the black velvet cushion, strapped down and spread-eagled, with Mr. Dark and Dangerous Dick between her thighs again.

"Now where did we leave off, firecat?" Darronn pressed his erection even tighter against her as he raised his head and studied her with his fiery green eyes. "Did you consider my words? Will you obey me without question?"

"I'm not someone you can order around." Alexi met his gaze straight on as her anger returned like flames devouring dry grass. Her voice rose as she hit her stride. "Do you get off on tying up someone smaller and weaker than you, and bullying them into submission?"

His expression shifted from sensual to hard in an instant. "It is clear you require more time to consider your lesson."

Alexi's stubbornness and pride kept her from shouting, *No! Don't leave me here!*

Instead she glared at him. "Go to hell."

Darronn smoothed his hands over her stocking-clad thighs as he eased back onto his haunches. He studied her, his muscles flexing and his jaw tightening. His deep voice was tightly controlled as he spoke. "When you can admit what you most desire and fear . . . when you show that you both trust and respect me . . . you will be free in mind, body, and spirit."

He backed away and stood, then waved his hand and the red shimmer filled the air again then vanished. Forest sounds and smells disappeared again—he'd encased her in some kind of protective bubble.

Darronn began to shift into a tiger and Alexi couldn't help but admire the amazing sight. It somehow made her feel small and insignificant, yet proud and powerful. When he was again a white tiger with black stripes, he studied her for a moment, and then she heard his voice in her head. *I am the only man who can make you whole. I am your Master.*

With beautiful, fluid movements, he loped out of her line of sight and into the strange blue-green mist.

Emotions raged through Alexi, as they had since the moment she walked into her town house and knew something had changed. She wasn't going to beat this man at his own game while strapped down and flat on her back. It was obvious he was just as stubborn as she was, and she'd have to change her game plan.

The beginnings of an idea glinted in the back of Alexi's mind. Darronn had said he wouldn't release her until she called him *Master*. All right, she'd do it, but once she was free, once she found the right opportunity, she'd get her revenge on him *and* escape.

Nobody screwed with Alexi O'Brien.

CHAPTER FOUR

WHEN DARRONN APPROACHED HIS MATE, IT was late in the afternoon. The protective shield he had placed around her had ensured the sun would not damage her perfect pale skin, and the wind would not chill her naked flesh.

He dismissed the shield and stepped between her thighs and looked down at her.

Alexi tilted her head and eyed him squarely. "Please free me now . . ." She swallowed, her throat working as though to choke back a name she felt more suitable to him than the one she must speak to free herself.

Darronn quirked one eyebrow and folded his arms across his chest. "Yes?"

The pain it caused her to say what she must was evident in her expression and in her tone. "Please free me, *Master*." She said "Master" in a way that sounded more like "bastard," but it pleased him nonetheless.

For this woman, such an admission was worth far more to him than any wench who threw herself at his feet and begged for his cock.

But he merely gave a single nod. "You have earned your freedom from your bindings . . . for now."

She bit her lip, her teeth white against the plump red flesh, as though trying to hold back a furious response. While he knelt between her thighs, her aqua eyes shot daggers at him—if they had been real, he would have been slain many times over.

Taking care to guard his bollocks, with a wave of his hand Darronn freed her using his magic, sending her ties and the stakes back to the château.

The sudden freedom took Alexi by surprise—she'd almost expected him to leave her there for another night. She didn't dare take her eyes from Darronn while she brought her aching arms down from over her head to her bare belly. Her bracelets were still melded together like manacles, and she was sore from being in the same position for almost an entire day. The only time she'd been up had been to pee, and that had been maybe ten minutes at the most.

"What are you going to do with me now?" she asked as he touched the bracelets with one finger. The gold separated, leaving her jewelry intact and as whole as they had been before.

Magic. He can do real magic.

"You will come with me to my château." Darronn rubbed her wrists with his strong fingers and worked

56

his way up her arms, and she wanted to melt into his touch. "There we shall sup and continue your training."

Rather than arguing with him, she braced her arms at her sides to push herself up, and he helped her to a sitting position. Now that she wasn't lying flat on her back, and wasn't dying to go to the bathroom—not as much, anyway—she got a good view of where she was. It was gorgeous, and reminded her of one of Annie's paintings. Better yet, that scene from *The Sound of Music* where the stepmom and all those kids were climbing over the beautiful mountains and singing.

Good grief. My mind has melted for sure.

Her heart dropped to her belly as she realized the magical mirror that she'd come through was gone.

She turned her gaze to Darronn and saw that the black eye she'd given him was even darker than before.

Ha. Serves him right. If she had the chance she'd blacken his other eye, too.

"Why are you doing this to me?" she asked.

Darronn shrugged, but the movement seemed anything but casual to her. "You are my destined mate."

"I don't belong here." Alexi winced as he massaged her aching muscles. She hated to admit it, but his hands felt wonderful. "And whatever you may think, I don't belong to you."

His expression remained calm as he continued to work her body with his magic touch. "This is your home, firecat."

"Damn it. You don't understand." Alexi's head ached

from not having her usual IV of caffeine and it took effort not to shout at him. "I have to find my sister. She disappeared a year ago, and if I don't go back home, I can't continue my search for her."

In a fluid movement, Darronn eased behind her and began massaging her neck and shoulders. "One day I will help you find this sister of yours."

Alexi couldn't help relaxing into his touch as he kneaded away the knots in her muscles. "At this point it will likely take a miracle to find Alice, but I won't stop until I do."

He paused for a long moment, his hands warm against her bare skin. "I am certain you will again be with your sister, firecat." His voice was firm and matter-of-fact, as if he believed what he said. "But first you must complete your training and realize your place is with me."

"Give me a break," she grumbled. She knew it was no use arguing the point with him. Not now, anyway.

After Darronn had finished massaging Alexi's muscles, he helped her to her feet. Her legs trembled and she wobbled on her heels. She would have fallen if he hadn't been there to hold her up. For just a fraction of time she allowed herself to lean into him, her naked breasts pressed against his clothed chest, his erection hard against her belly, his hands holding her hips.

His warm, earthy scent filled her sense. She clenched her hands in his tunic and raised her face to look into those hungry untamed eyes of his. Damn, but she wanted him, and Alexi O'Brien always went after what she wanted.

She was tall, but he was a good foot taller than her, even when she wore stilettos. A rumble rose within his chest as Alexi reached up and slid her arms around his neck and tried to pull his head down to hers while she stood on her toes. She wanted to kiss him. *Needed* it.

He didn't budge. He only studied her with that intense gaze of his.

Alexi scowled and turned away. "I've got to pee," she said as she stomped off and found another bush. It ticked her off even more that he followed her, but what else could she expect from the bastard who had kidnapped her?

After she relieved herself, Darronn led her back to the meadow. The stakes, the cushion, her scraps of clothing . . . all of it was gone. Apparently he'd used his magic again to get rid of it all.

Darronn raised his head and gave a sharp cry—like a call of some sort. In the next moment she heard a thundering sound, and then a creature tore from the depths of the forest. He was a beautiful silver beast—like a horse, but different. His muzzle was much narrower and his coat had a lustrous sheen to it, like a pool of liquid silver. As he galloped toward them, his movements were as smooth and fluid as Darronn's when he was a tiger.

When the creature reached them and came to a stop, he lowered his head and butted Darronn lightly on the shoulder.

Darronn rubbed his knuckles along the creature's muzzle. "My good friend Tok of the *jul,* I have a favor to ask of you this day. A ride for my mate Alexi and me, if you please."

Fascinated, Alexi watched the beast toss his head and murmur a reply in a tone that was almost human.

"Many thanks, Tok." Darronn inclined his head and released Alexi's waist. From out of nowhere he produced a satiny black saddle blanket along with a black leather saddle—like magic—and settled both onto Tok's back.

He moved behind Alexi and gripped her waist. Before she even had a chance to think, he was lifting her into the air, and she gave a small shout of surprise. As if she was light as a doll, he easily placed her on the saddle, close to Tok's neck. The leather saddle felt exciting and erotic between her naked thighs and against her smooth slit. Tok's fine hair was like silk to her fingertips as she gripped his silver mane, and he smelled of warm buttermilk biscuits and honey.

Her stomach growled.

After he helped Alexi mount Tok, the horselike beast that he'd called a *jul*, Darronn swung up behind her. He pulled her toward him so that her back was snug to his chest, her ass tight between his thighs and his hard cock. His arms were around her waist, the spade tattoo on his wrist seeming to almost glitter in the sunshine.

"We will dine as soon as we reach my château," he said.

Alexi allowed herself to relax against Darronn's muscular length as the *jul* began to move in the direction of the waterfall. Blue-green mist that had been there in the morning had apparently burned away like San Francisco fog on a sunny day. The sun clung to the mountaintops, its golden light spilling over the top of the forest.

This place and this man must be getting to her, because it felt like the most natural thing in the world to be wearing only her thigh-high nylons and stiletto heels. Not to mention being positioned between Darronn's legs with her thighs spread wide, while riding a silver horse called a *jul*. It was kind of like riding her Harley, only naked.

Yup. She was losing it, all right.

Wind chilled her nipples and her exposed folds, and Tok's rolling gait didn't help the ache in her pussy any. Alexi shifted, tempted to slide her fingers into her slit and take care of that ache right now.

"You feel perfect in my arms," Darronn murmured near her ear, his coarse stubble brushing her skin and causing a thrill to skitter through her. He moved his hands over her breasts and she couldn't help but moan as he pinched and pulled her nipples, making her even hotter than she already was.

Alexi slid her fingers down to her clit and into her core and almost came at once.

"No, firecat." Darronn brought his arms all the way around her and captured her wrists in his hands. He leaned back, bringing her wrists behind her and then magically fastened her gold bracelets together again. "You may not climax without my permission."

"Damn you," she muttered as he pulled her against

61

his chest, except this time he had her hands trapped between them. Yet even as she cursed at him, she felt hornier than ever.

As the horse-beast moved into the trees on a sun-dappled trail, Darronn held his palm out in front of Alexi. On it a strange device appeared, as if it had just popped out onto his hand. It looked a lot like the spade tattoo on his wrist, only three-dimensional.

Alexi frowned. "What are you going to do with that?"

"A teaching tool," Darronn murmured as he lowered it.

He had his other arm wrapped tight around her waist, and her arms were bound behind her, so she had no choice but to watch as he lowered it between her thighs.

Her heart beat faster and blood rushed in her head as the unusually warm tip penetrated her core. The sides folded down as he slid it inside her all the way—and then the spade expanded.

"Oh, jeez." Alexi gasped as the device filled her, and then she almost screamed with pleasure as it started to vibrate.

Tok the horse-beast continued on as though Alexi wasn't getting the ride of her life, the soft clip-clop of his hooves moving in time to the spade thrusting in and out of her core, seemingly of its own volition. Likely the bastard behind her was using his magic to make it move that way.

When did she start taking *magic* for granted?

"Do not climax without my permission," Darronn

ordered, even as she rushed toward an orgasm. "Or you will be punished."

Screw you. She'd come whenever she wanted, and no one was going to punish her.

Closer and closer her orgasm built. Just as she thought she was going to come, the spade vibrator stopped. It shrank within her core and Alexi almost cried out in frustration.

Darronn's palm was warm against her belly, and he flicked the tiger charm at her navel with one finger. "Ask permission if you wish to climax, wench."

"Fuck you," she responded.

He gave a low and vibrant chuckle. "Soon enough, my firecat."

It started again. The spade expanded and began vibrating and moving up and down. It felt as though a cock thrust inside her while thickening, driving her wild with the need to come. Sweat broke out over her skin, and her breathing grew heavier.

Darronn flicked his tongue along her neck while playing with her nipples and she arched toward him even more. "Ask permission," he demanded.

She tightened her lips. "No."

The vibrator stopped again and Alexi, who never cried, wanted to weep.

"We are near the village." He pinched and pulled at her nipples. "If you wish to climax before we arrive, then ask."

Alexi gritted her teeth. Like hell she'd ask for permission. She'd just wait until she was alone and take care of the matter herself. Maybe even Tok's gait would get her off. The feel of the beast between her naked thighs, the world's best vibrator in her core, and her bare folds and breasts . . . She was so damn horny maybe she'd come if a good stiff breeze hit her clit.

The ride got a little bumpier the higher they climbed. The spade remained lodged in her core, but didn't move. The terrain became more mountainous and beautiful with its strange-looking trees—some with glossy trunks and blue feathers for leaves, and others with foliage like lace doilies or snowflakes.

When it hit her that Darronn had said they were nearing a village, her heart rate picked up again. "You're not going to make me ride through the village like . . . like Lady Godiva?"

"It is your choice." Darronn lifted her hair and kissed the back of her neck, where tendrils were damp from sweat. "Ask me for what you need. Whether it is clothing or pleasure, I will consider your request."

She pressed her lips tight and stared into the trees ahead. Waning sunlight flickered through the treetops and she thought she heard voices.

The spade toy expanded in her pussy again and started vibrating.

Oh, God. She couldn't take much more of this. Although it was killing her, she could wait for her orgasm, but she couldn't wait to be clothed. Even though the idea of riding through a village in only her thigh-highs and stilettos turned her on in some bizarre way, she couldn't get past the thought of it being wrong to be naked in

public. For men and women to see her bound and naked, her breasts jutting forward, her nipples hard, and
her legs spread wide.

And a vibrator in her core.

The spade's movements seemed to grow even more
intense, more frantic, pushing her closer and closer to
orgasm so that she couldn't speak. But what if she climaxed without his permission and he refused to give
her clothing as punishment?

Now she fought against coming, needing something
to wear, even though her body told her she needed to
climax more than anything. "P-please, may I have something to wear?" she forced out, hating the fact that she
was stuttering. Hating the fact that she had to ask for
what she needed.

"How must you refer to me?" he asked, and at the
same time she was sure she heard laughter coming from
around a turn in the road.

No! She wasn't going to call him Master again. She'd
only done it the first time so that he'd untie her. But this
was different.

"It is your choice, wench," he murmured, and the timbre of his voice almost threw her over the edge. She
needed to be fucked so badly that she almost didn't care
who saw her right now, or what they might say.

"I am your Master now, Alexi." His voice urged her
to comply, demanded it of her. "Your training will go
much easier if you acknowledge it now."

The spade continued to move in and out of her
core, filling her as the horse-beast neared the sounds of

tools clanking, voices chatting, and wheels rattling over rocks.

Alexi didn't give a damn who saw her anymore. She'd rather be seen naked in the streets of this village, a place where she didn't intend to be for long, than give Darronn the satisfaction of bowing down to him.

"Say it," he urged her.

"Screw . . . you," she managed to get out just before the most intense climax of her life ripped through her.

She screamed and Darronn clenched his hand in her hair, jerked her head to the side, and claimed her lips in a rough and brutal kiss. And she wanted it even harder from him. Heat from her orgasm flushed through her from head to toe in wave after wave after wave and she didn't want it to end. The spade's vibrations grew wilder yet and she climaxed again and then again.

Darronn tore his lips from hers, his breathing hard, and his eyes glazed, as if he could barely contain himself. Vaguely she felt his hand between her thighs and he slipped the spade out. She turned her gaze from his to see the device on his palm, and then it vanished.

"You have earned your next punishment." His tone was a mixture of frustration, anger, and lust. "Now ask for what you need before we enter the village."

Village? What the hell. She'd just had the best orgasm of her life. She sighed and relaxed against Darronn's chest, still riding smaller waves of pleasure.

Sounds of people and industry were louder now, and soon everyone would see her spread out like a woman who had just been screwed. Her skin was flushed and covered in a fine sheen of sweat, her breasts were swollen with need, her nipples hard and erect, her hands bound behind her back.

And she was about to be paraded through a village.

Bring it on.

CHAPTER FIVE

THE RAPTURE ON ALEXI'S FACE AS SHE CLImaxed over and over again had almost caused Darronn to spill his seed into his breeches. He wished only to spell away the leather, lift up his mate and slam her down onto his cock, and drive into her until she screamed her pleasure again.

Although Darronn relished the thought of dealing out the punishment for climaxing without his permission, a punishment he was sure his new queen would enjoy, he could not believe her stubbornness. As it grew more apparent that she would rather be seen naked in the streets of Spades than to call him Master, his frustration mounted.

Although nakedness or near nakedness was commonplace in all of Tarok, including Spades, Darronn had no desire for anyone to view his mate's treasures but him. The possessiveness took him by surprise and nearly shocked him speechless.

He was tempted to guide Tok away from the village and fuck Alexi to their mutual oblivion. It would be well into the night then, and the darkness would be a fine cloak when he took her to his château.

Or perhaps he should retrieve clothing for her now. She had asked, she simply had not addressed him in a respectful manner, as a submissive mate should.

"Ask," he hissed.

"Nope." And then the wench pressed her bound palms against his cock and, as much as her position would allow, skimmed her fingers along its contours.

Darronn bit back a growl and a groan.

"Very well," he said between clenched teeth. "It is your choice, wench."

"Sure is," she said in a voice that taunted him, as though she knew he wished for anything but her delectable breasts and quim to be viewed by his people.

Darronn straightened in his seat and urged Tok forward. He was king, damn the skies. And he never backed down on his word.

When they entered the village, embarrassment flushed over Alexi, but she kept her chin high. While bowing to their king, men and women openly appraised her, obviously enjoying the sight of her naked body while Darronn gave rumbling snarls that almost made her laugh out loud. His little plan had backfired on him, and she knew it.

Alexi was still incredibly relaxed from her once-in-a-lifetime cataclysmic orgasm. She felt drugged from it . . . and drugged from the power she now knew she held over Darronn. She smiled at the people and would have waved if her hands weren't bound behind her back. Their appreciative stares made her body come back to life, and soon she was hornier than ever. Especially after getting a glimpse of what the villagers in this place wore. Big, brawny men in tight leather shirts and pants, and the women in strips of leather that showed more skin than they covered.

Darronn let out a low rumble and Tok trotted faster. Alexi had to bite her lip to keep from giggling, and she never giggled unless she was drunk.

One thing she noticed was that his people did not look at him with fear, or with reverence as if he was some kind of god. Instead they smiled and appeared open and friendly, as if they were used to him working right beside them. Yet she could clearly see their respect for their king, too.

The village reminded her of a cross between a medieval setting and something more fantastical. Carts laden with produce, hay, and things Alexi didn't recognize, traveled along the wide street . . . but with no obvious means of locomotion. No horses, no motors, no person even guiding them. Vendors stood behind boxes of fruits and vegetables that hovered without support, and unusual objects appeared and disappeared at random.

The road was paved with flagstones and all kinds of shops lined each side. Everything was clean and well kept and it smelled wonderful . . . of fresh baked bread from a bakery, roasted meats from a street vendor, and ale from a tavern. Her stomach rumbled again, and she realized it had been a good day since her huge meal and night out with Annie.

At the thought of her cousin, her smile turned into a frown. If Alexi didn't get back to her soon, Annie would freak. She was calm and quiet, a real southern lady, but she could get riled in a hurry if people she loved were in trouble.

When Alice had vanished, Annie had searched for her as hard as anyone. Even though Annie had told Alexi she needed to get on with her life, she knew better than to believe that her cousin would follow her own advice. In her own quiet way, Annie would continue the search for Alice and never give up. And if Alexi didn't make it back . . . damn. Annie might even blame herself for not walking Alexi into the house and making sure it was locked up tight.

And of course Aunt Awai would go ballistic. Never mind Alexi's administrative assistant, Angie, who also happened to be a friend.

Nope, not even going to consider not getting back home. Alexi never let down the people she loved.

When they were beyond the admiring stares of the villagers, Alexi was almost disappointed. She could understand how models and movie stars enjoyed showing off their assets to the public—it made her hotter than ever. And best of all, it had made Darronn crazy.

As Tok carried them from the village and climbed higher on the mountain, Alexi caught glimpses of a massive earth-toned structure through the trees. It blended into the mountainside, like an incredibly huge work of art.

"Did it please you to have my people look upon your body?" Darronn asked in a furious tone, breaking into her thoughts.

Holding back a laugh, Alexi replied, "And what if it did?"

Darronn's voice deepened. "You *will* learn to respond to me in a manner befitting your station."

Alexi rolled her eyes. "Get off it already."

He actually growled. "Your punishments continue to grow."

"Whatever." She was too damn light-headed and hungry to argue with him right now, and she was afraid that he was going to make her beg for food. She could just see it now, her dying of starvation because he was too stubborn to stop trying to make her call him Master.

And she was too stubborn to give in.

When they finally broke through the cover of trees, she could clearly see the château spilling down the hillside, flowing with the terrain. She straightened in her seat, pulling away from Darronn as she absorbed the most beautiful place she'd ever seen.

"It's gorgeous," she said aloud, without meaning to.

"Welcome to Spades." Pride filled Darronn's voice. "Your new home."

She ignored the comment and instead concentrated on the terraced gardens, the balconies and large windows that must give a breathtaking view of his realm.

When they reached the point, at the highest floor of the building, Darronn guided Tok to what she thought must be a stable. Unusual animal sounds came from the stable, like the sounds Tok had made upon occasion during the ride to the château.

Darronn swung off Tok's back then pulled Alexi off in a quick movement, her hands still bound behind her. He spun her around and clasped one hand on her ass cheek, forcing her tightly to him, while his other hand cupped the back of her head and held her still. "You are a stubborn wench," he said in a fierce growl, his green eyes blazing as though lit with fire from within.

She met his gaze head-on. "And you're a stubborn ass."

Darronn brought her roughly to him at the same moment he lowered his mouth to hers. His lips crushed hers, and her head spun with the thrill and excitement of the barely contained power raging through him.

He was furious with her, but he wouldn't hurt her, she was absolutely certain. Her instincts had never failed her. King Darronn might be a bad boy, but he was a good man . . . who just happened to want to get his way all the time.

Well, he'd met his match in Alexi O'Brien, and if he hadn't figured that one out, he was sure to in a hurry.

Darronn pulled away from her and snarled. With a roar he threw Alexi over his shoulder and strode toward his château and his quarters. The anger and lust burning through Darronn was beyond anything he had felt in his almost two hundred and forty Tarok years.

"Neanderthal!" Alexi wiggled against his back and shouted, "Put me down!"

He positioned his arms just beneath Alexi's ass so that her quim would not be seen by the residents of his château. With his mate over his shoulder, her breasts and mons were covered, away from curious gazes. He no longer questioned why he felt such desire to keep his future queen as his own. She belonged to him, and never again would he share her in any manner. In the presence of others, she would always remain clothed.

The sound of Darronn's boots rang out against the polished black granite as he strode down steps that led him through the magnificent beveled-glass and wood doors, the wood carved from the finest *ch'tok* trees. Alexi continued to order him to put her down, and before any of his servants could hear her, he swatted her naked ass with the flat of his free hand.

She yelped and moaned all in one breath, and Darronn's cock was surely going to explode. Torches lit his way as his long strides ate up the endless hallway of polished black granite that led to his quarters. Servants remained scarce, apparently sensing his foul mood. Darronn had never harmed any subject within his realm and he never would. Nevertheless, when his mood was dark, those in his employ stayed clear.

When he finally reached his quarters, Darronn shoved the doors open with his magic and used it again to slam the heavy wood shut behind him. He slipped Alexi from his shoulder and tossed her into the middle of his bed.

Alexi landed on her back, her legs splayed, her eyes wide, her lips parted, and her hands still bound behind her back.

Growling, Darronn paced the floor at the foot of the carved wooden bed. He *had* to regain control. He could not allow this wench to gain the upper hand on him in any way.

With a twist of his fingers in the air, he used his magic to release the binding he'd placed on her bracelets.

"About time." She pushed herself up so that her freed hands now braced her, but she didn't close her silk-clad thighs. Instead she tossed back her head and waited, as if daring him to slide between those thighs and take her.

"You have earned more punishments, wench," he said as he continued pacing.

"You don't get it, do you?" Alexi rose so that she was on her hands and knees, moving to the edge of the bed, toward him, in a slow feline crawl, and he came to an abrupt stop. Her breasts swayed, almost mesmerizing him with their movements, and her tiger charm dangled from her navel. "I don't care what you think, or what you do to me. I will bow to no man."

"In that you are greatly mistaken." Darronn strode to Alexi and grabbed a handful of her auburn hair and held her head in front of his furious erection. "If I order you to suck my cock, you will."

"No." She shook her head and her mouth brushed

against his leather breeches, making him think she might intentionally be doing it to drive him mad.

"If I order you to lie on your belly so that I may take you from behind, you will do so."

"Nope." Alexi skimmed her tongue along the outline of his erection, and despite himself his cock jerked in his breeches. "I'll do it only if it's because that's what *I* want."

Darronn grabbed Alexi's waist. In a quick movement he sat on the bed and had her settled across his lap. She gasped and tried to move, but he had her positioned so that her ass was up in the air, her arms and hair hanging over her head. He slid his fingers between her thighs and forced them apart so that he could see her folds. Her warm scent nearly drove him to take her, damn the training.

"Let me up, Conan." She struggled and pounded at his boot-covered calf. "Ow. What's that thing made of—steel?"

Alexi wasn't sure what Darronn was going to do to her, but she had a good idea that he was going to spank her . . . and she hoped he would. She was already wetter at the thought, and struggling against him, acting like she didn't want it, was turning her on even more. The masterful way he handled her was sexually exciting, and not demeaning at all—not like calling him Master would be. That was pushing things too far.

She moaned as he rubbed her ass with his palm. "What will it take to teach you your rightful place, fire-cat?"

"I'm your equal, Darronn." She squirmed in his lap, feeling the hard press of his cock against her hip. "When are you going to realize you can't control me?"

"Do you understand why I am punishing you?" he asked, his callused hand stroking her ass cheeks in a slow, rhythmic movement.

"Just do it already." Alexi arched her hips up toward his hand. "And then fuck me."

A sharp inhalation, as if she'd thrown him for a loop, and then his hand smacked her ass. Hard.

Alexi shouted, more from the surprise than from the sting. Before she had a chance to catch her breath, he swatted her again and again, each time in a different location.

The sensations were wild and unexpected. She'd been turned on by the *thought* of being sexually spanked by a powerful man, but she'd never imagined it would be like this. His swats smarted, but each sting turned into immediate warmth that spread over her ass cheeks and straight to her pussy.

Just when she was about to come, Darronn flipped her off his lap and onto her back on the bed. A glaze of passion and need filled her vision, and she prayed that he was going to drive his cock into her. But instead he slid his palms beneath her stinging ass cheeks and lowered his face.

Alexi nearly came unglued as he paused and took a deep breath, as though drinking in the rich scent of her. "I want your cock inside me, Darronn."

He dipped his tongue into her core and she cried out, arching into him. "Such a sweet, sweet taste," he murmured, as though lost in the moment. Then he laved her in one long stroke from core to mound.

She shouted again and grabbed his head, clenching her hands in his hair as if that might allow her to hold him there until he finished the job. Darronn only paused a moment, perhaps warring with himself for giving her any control at all. But then he pressed his face against her folds and sucked on her clit.

A shriek tore from Alexi, so loud and so long, that it was a wonder the windows didn't shatter. Her hips jerked against him as her orgasm nearly split her in two. Darronn gave a growl of satisfaction as he continued to press against her, to force her to another orgasm, then another.

She struggled against him, trying to get him to stop. The pleasure was too exquisite, too much to take. She'd thought the spade had been unbelievable, but Darronn's mouth took her even further, until he finally let her go.

While he watched his mate recover from her many orgasms, he studied her flushed face and body, the heavy rise and fall of her chest, the fluids drenching her folds. The need to take her was beyond any need he remembered ever experiencing in his life.

Control. This was about him gaining control of his woman.

His need for her was so great he had to obtain release

now. If it had been any other wench than Alexi that he endeavored to train, he would have sought out Kalina or any one of the servants, like the voluptuous Kira. In the past he would have taken several wenches at once. But now that he had found Alexi, he could no longer think of himself with any other woman in any way. It occurred to him that now he understood why Jarronn would only enjoy Alice's pleasures.

For Darronn would have no woman but Alexi in his bed.

He kept his gaze focused on her glazed aqua eyes as he unfastened his breeches. He didn't dare spell his clothing away, or the feel of his bare skin against hers would surely drive him to take her. Not that clothing could stop him.

Darronn climbed onto the bed and straddled Alexi, pulling out his cock at the same time as he neared her face. Her eyes grew wide, and he heard her murmur something that sounded like, "Ohmygod," and "King Kong."

Before she had a chance to deny him with words, he placed his cock to her mouth. She parted her lips and he slid into her wet warmth.

Alexi took him deeper than he had expected, her eyes focused on him while her tongue swirled around the head of his cock and she applied strong suction. She brought her hands up and wrapped one around the base of his cock, and cradled his bollocks with the other. With any of his women in the past, he would never have allowed them to use their hands without his permission. He demanded total submission and complete control.

But Alexi . . . what in the name of the skies was she doing to him?

She made soft moans as she sucked him, and her eyes told him how much she enjoyed his cock in her mouth. He braced his hands on the bed, above her head, determined to take more control, and started thrusting his hips harder and faster in and out of her mouth.

The need for his woman had built to such incredible proportions that his climax slammed into him like an avalanche roaring down from a Tarok Mountain peak. He bellowed as he came, his shout loud enough to thunder through his château. His fluid spurted into the back of Alexi's throat as she sucked him and sucked him, until he pulled his wet and still firm cock out of her mouth.

She licked at a drop of his fluid that had dribbled down the corner of her mouth. "I need your cock in me, Darronn. Now."

He shook his head and eased away from her until he stood at the foot of the bed. "A bath will be drawn for you and dinner shall be served in these quarters."

Darronn ignored the lust and surprise in her eyes, and fastened his breeches as he strode toward the doors. He shoved the wooden doors open with his hands, but used his magic to close and lock them tight so that his future queen could not escape.

After leaving Alexi, Darronn shifted into a tiger and loped down the long hallways of his château, his paws silent against the granite floor. He slipped away from his home and into the darkening forest and prowled through the *ch'tok* and *sini* trees. He made not a sound as he slipped between bushes and bounded over crystal streams. His gaze took in all that surrounded him, and his sensitive hearing caught every sound, from the chirrup of crickets to the scamper of mice among the forest's damp leaves.

His thoughts turned toward Alexi's concern for her missing sister. Should he tell her that Alice was now High Queen of Tarok and the Queen of Hearts?

A rumble rose up in his chest. If he did it was likely she would want to leave immediately, making it far more difficult to convince her that her place was with him in Spades. No, he would wait until the appropriate time, when he decided it was the moment for her to know.

In all Darronn's years, never had he known such a frustrating and stubborn woman as Alexi. She defied him at every turn. She reveled in her defiance, even.

Within his soul, he knew that Alexi's heart needed to heal from past wounds—he sensed it as clearly as if she had told him aloud. He knew that she needed to give control to him so that she would no longer feel as though she must take on the world.

But how will I convince her of that?

He had already shown weakness with her. As any good Tarok King or Master would, he should become stricter, should rein the wench in and keep her under tighter control.

Yet even as those thoughts crossed his mind, he pictured Alexi refusing him at every turn. With his physical and magical superiority, he could force her to bow down to him, could take everything away from her until she gave in to his demands.

But he did not wish to force her. He wanted her to experience enjoyment, not anger or frustration, or pain beyond what was exciting and pleasurable. No doubt her fiery spirit would not allow her to be dominated.

Do I want to break that spirit?

Shaking his large head, Darronn gave a low growl and plunged deeper into the forest. No, he did not wish to break her. He reveled in his future queen's passionate nature, admired all that he had seen of her.

How, then, to train her to serve at my side?

"Compromise" was the word that came to his mind, but it did not easily come to his tongue. He was King of Spades, damn the skies, and his subjects followed his orders without question.

However, Alexi was not his subject, and had not been raised in the ways of his world. She would be his queen, not his servant. Could, perhaps, different rules apply to her?

He was king. He made the rules in his kingdom.

Alexi had asked for clothing when he demanded it of her, but she had refused to call him Master. Was it enough that she asked for what it was that she wanted, without referring to him in such a manner?

With the grace of his species, Darronn bounded over several felled trees and caught the scent of an *anlia* buck nearby. His belly roared with hunger and his predatory senses kicked in. Perhaps a hunt and a good feed would clear his mind.

It was late into the night when Darronn returned to his quarters, still in his tiger form. He spelled the doors open and quietly closed them behind him again with his magic. Immediately he caught the scent of Alexi's feminine musk among the more customary smells of bathing gels, oils, and wood burning in his hearth.

The room was dark, save for a slice of moonlight spilling through a gap in the heavy draperies, and the orange glow of embers in the fireplace. With his keen feline vision, light was not necessary.

He padded silently to the bedside to see Alexi asleep, her features relaxed and a smile teasing the corner of her mouth. Her reddish-brown hair tumbled about her face and he sniffed at her clean skin and the almond-scented shampoo and body gel she must have used during her bath. A light blanket was loosely draped over her form, exposing her bare shoulder and back, and the curve of one breast.

Need that had never dissipated grew even fiercer as he watched his woman sleeping. No, he would not take her until he felt she was ready—no matter that she had already invited him inside of her.

With a sigh of frustration, Darronn stretched out on the floor beside the bed and rested his head on his paws.

It would be a long night, indeed.

CHAPTER SIX

ALEXI SNUGGLED INTO THE FUR COVERING and gave a contented sigh. She felt warm and loved and safe, as if she was being hugged by a giant teddy bear. The ache in her head from her caffeine withdrawal had lessened and her knuckles didn't throb any more.

She lifted her eyelids to see that she was in Darronn's bed in his enormous bedroom. She was lying on her side, facing the fireplace. The fire had died down during the night, leaving only a few glowing coals.

When she'd gone to bed she'd been naked, not bothering to slip on the covering that Kira, a servant, had left when she'd drawn the bath. The honey-blond-haired woman seemed to take pleasure in serving Alexi, and in being subservient. Judging by her sensual movements, Kira obviously relished wearing her skimpy leather outfit that exposed more boob than it hid.

While Alexi had bathed, Kira had gently washed out

the thigh-high stockings, and cleaned the dirt off the red stilettos, then put them away in a trunk filled with leather clothing.

Another pair of servants had served Alexi's meal, which had actually been quite good. The food was different—breads, vegetables, and pastries she wasn't familiar with—but she had never been squeamish and she'd been starving, so she dug in.

She'd been too hungry to talk, and by the time she finished dinner and climbed into her bath all the servants had vanished, so she'd never had a chance to ask any questions. After her bath, she'd toweled off and tried opening the doors to the balcony and to the hallway, but everything had been locked.

It had been a long day, and she was tired, so she'd crawled into bed and had fallen asleep in no time.

Alexi sighed as her thoughts turned to Darronn. Last night she'd been so hot for him. He'd licked her clit and had given her such spectacular orgasms, then she'd sucked him off and he'd left.

She snuggled deeper into the fur and smiled. Yeah, she'd been disappointed. She couldn't deny how much she wanted Darronn. But she also knew that she had some power over him, even if he'd never admit it.

A yawn escaped her and she started to roll onto her back, only to realize that something very large, very warm, and very immovable was directly behind her. And a massive white paw was draped over her shoulder. A paw with a stripe in a black spade design.

She scooted away from Tony the Tiger enough to roll over in his feline embrace so that she was facing him.

Darronn's vibrant green eyes were open and studying her. Even in his tiger form, his eyes were expressive, telling her more than he wanted her to know, she was certain. He didn't know what to do with her. She wasn't fitting the mold of every other woman he'd ever known.

Alexi couldn't help the smile that curved her lips as she raised her hand to stroke the soft white fur of his muzzle. "Good morning, Darronn."

And to you, my firecat. A rumble rose in his chest and his pink tongue darted out and licked the tip of her nose, and she laughed.

"I know you think I belong here with you. But I don't. I have a home back in San Francisco, and more importantly, I have a sister to search for." Somehow it seemed easier talking to him when he was big, soft, furry, and cuddly. "And I'm not the submissive type. I'm not right for you."

In this you are wrong. Darronn the tiger purred and then transformed . . . Beneath her fingertips white fur changed to olive skin and dark brown hair. The fur on his body melted away, his body morphing, muscles shifting.

In moments Darronn the man was in her arms, his naked body only inches from hers. Her fingers now caressed his stubbled jaw to his ear and into his wild brown hair. His gold earring and the black eye she'd given him almost made him look like a pirate.

"You're magnificent," she said as she touched him. "As a tiger or a man."

"You are the perfect woman for me." Darronn slipped one hand into her hair, cupped the back of her head, and brought his lips close until they barely hovered over hers. "I will have no other."

The look in Darronn's eyes and the depth of feeling in his voice was almost more than Alexi could handle. She never allowed any man to get under her skin, and she wasn't going to let this one, either. What she needed was a good fuck, and this was the guy who could give it to her.

Besides, if she didn't solve her immediate lust problem, she wouldn't be able to get her mind back on escaping, and then to finding her way back to San Francisco and searching for her sister.

Instead of waiting for Darronn to kiss her, Alexi clenched her hand in his hair and brought her lips up to meet his. She lightly bit his lower lip and he growled, the sound rumbling through her body and straight through her.

The kiss became a whirlwind of sensation and feeling, their tongues thrusting and tasting. His stubble chafed her mouth, her chin, her lips, and she moaned from the erotic sensations. Alexi wanted Darronn more than any man she'd ever known. She wanted his body tight to hers, wanted his cock deep inside her.

As for birth control, she'd had the hormone implant inserted under the skin of her upper arm a while back because she loved sex but didn't want to have to worry about getting pregnant and interrupting her career. It had been far too long since she'd had a man, though, and she'd *never* had a man like this one.

Darronn moved his hand from her hair, slid it down to her ass, and pressed their bodies tightly together. His cock was so hard and so enormous it felt as if it was bruising her belly. Her nipples brushed against his chest, making the ache in her pussy even greater.

While they continued ravaging each other, Alexi hooked one leg over his hips and tried to push him on to his back so that she could climb on top and ride him. But he was too powerful, and instead he rolled her onto her back and positioned himself between her thighs.

He tore his mouth from hers and looked down at her with savage intensity in his green eyes. "In my bed, you are mine to command, firecat."

Her many fantasies came back to her, a secret thrill that made her even hornier. "In bed only?" she asked as her eyes met his, and she knew her gaze held a challenge.

"There are many things I wish to do that would give you pleasure beyond your dreams." He pressed his erection against her slit. "But you need to relinquish control to me."

The fact that he was asking—in his own way—was enough to give Alexi pause, and it excited her, too. Here was a man used to total submission from his women, yet willing to keep it in the bedroom for her. Being mastered sexually had been her fantasy for a long time, and this was the only man she could ever imagine submitting to.

Oooh, like the fantasy she'd had about being a French maid being erotically punished by her employer. Or better yet, where she was a servant in a palace where the prince had to sexually punish her for misbehaving. . . .

"I *have* been a bad, bad serving girl." She ran her tongue along her lower lip and enjoyed watching the flare of desire in his eyes. "How will you punish me . . . Master?"

Surprise, then raging lust washed over his expression, both replaced by a mask of control. The face of a king who ruled his kingdom with a firm hand. That power was such a turn-on and it added fuel to her fantasy.

Darronn moved from between her thighs and knelt on the bed, his massive chest muscles flexing and his hair wild about his shoulders—and his cock thrusting out in the biggest hard-on she'd ever seen in her life.

"You require discipline for ignoring your duties to your king." He raised his arm, the one with the spade tattoo, and a black leather strap appeared in his palm. "On your knees, wench."

The way he said *wench . . . damn,* but it was sexy. Alexi grew even wetter. What he had in mind for that strap she wasn't sure, but from what she'd come to know about Darronn, she trusted him not to hurt her. In fact, she was certain she would enjoy whatever he came up with. Nearly breathless with anticipation, she raised herself up on her knees so that she was facing him. "What would you have me do now, Master?"

"Widen your thighs and turn toward the wall." While

she complied, Darronn trailed the strap over her breasts, causing her nipples to harden. "Stretch your body forward and place your hands upon the bar," he instructed, gesturing to the headboard's wood railing.

Alexi complied, a sensual shiver racing throughout her body. When she had a firm grip on the bar, Darronn moved closer and then tied her hands to it with the black leather strap.

Her breathing grew even more rapid and her skin tingled with anticipation. She glanced at Darronn and saw that he held a black cloth. Before she could gather her thoughts enough to wonder what he had in mind for it, he was tying it around her head, blindfolding her. "How are you going to punish me, Master?" she asked, hardly able to stand the wait.

"In addition to your disobedience, you talk far too much for a serving girl." Darronn's tone was so sensual that Alexi knew he was getting off on this as much as she was. Being blindfolded made her even more aware of his musky smell, the heat of his body, the need in his voice. "This should solve the immediate problem of your insolence."

Alexi gasped as a silk cloth was slipped between her lips and tied around her head. She made a sound of protest and tugged against her bonds, but the effort was only halfhearted. It was unbelievable to have her knees splayed wide and cool air skimming her folds, her hands bound to the bed, to be blindfolded and gagged—and totally at his mercy.

She felt the soft caress of leather over her ass cheeks and a trickle of fear and excitement filled her.

"In my kingdom my servants must perform their duties with efficiency." The leather strap moved up her backside, along her spine to her neck, and then across each shoulder. "You have been neglecting your duties, wench," Darronn murmured, "and for that you will be punished."

The strap moved over her back while she felt something being pressed into her hand. It felt soft and rubbery, and of the same shape as the spade vibrator. "Drop the spade if you feel anything but pleasure," he murmured near her ear. "If you feel fear, or wish me to stop, just release it and this game ends."

Ha! Alexi O'Brien never backs down from a challenge.

Darronn growled and she shivered. "Nod if you understand, wench."

Alexi swallowed behind her gag and nodded.

A snapping sound, like a whip, and then a sting against her ass cheeks startled Alexi into crying out behind the gag and nearly dropping the spade. The sting quickly melted into warmth that spread across her skin.

"You turn a lovely shade of pink for me, wench," he murmured, and another lash fell.

She clenched the spade tighter and the next lash fell and then the next. It seemed that the more he lashed her, the better it felt. The pain turned into a kind of rapture she had never expected. Soon she was pressing back, moving into the lashes, and moaning from the sheer excitement and the heat now radiating all over her body. He lashed her shoulders, her back, her ass, her thighs, always continuing to another location and never striking in the same place twice.

But what shocked Alexi more than anything was how close she was to orgasm. It seemed that every strike of his strap made her hornier and hornier yet.

"Remember that you may not climax without my permission, wench," Darronn said as he continued the erotic punishment. "If you do, I shall be forced to punish you yet again."

Alexi wasn't sure she could handle much more pleasure and pain than this. And since they were playing at him being her Master, then she would do whatever it took to hold back her orgasm. Any challenge she put her mind to, she would win.

Darronn laid the strap across her back as he moved behind her, between her splayed thighs, and she almost sighed with relief. She needed to come so badly she was on the fine, fine edge.

But when he grasped her butt cheeks and she felt his rough tongue lave her folds, she almost lost it. Small tremors caused her thighs to quiver. She fought against her bonds and shouted at him to stop, but her gag held back the scream.

He gave a satisfied sound and thankfully moved away. But then he growled in his tigerlike way and bit her ass cheek hard enough to bring tears to her eyes.

Marking her.

"You belong to me, Alexi." Darronn grabbed her slim hips in his large hands and pressed his erection to her ass.

She pulled against her bonds and clenched the spade tighter. She wanted to talk, to tell him that she was his for now, only in this bed, and just for this moment, but the gag held her words back and the blindfold kept her from trying to look over her shoulder to tell him with her eyes.

The rough scrape of his stubble against the already sensitive skin of her back sent sparks flying through her body. "Do you deny me?" he murmured.

All she wanted in this world right now was for Darronn to slide his cock into her, and to take her hard. She shook her head, answering his question, and hoping he understood her answer.

Darronn gave a purr of satisfaction, a deep tiger's rumble. He straightened behind her and she felt him placing his cock at the entrance to her core. She pressed against him, trying to take him deeper, but he pulled back.

"I am your Master." He retrieved the strap he'd left lying across her back and swatted her ass with it. "I determine when and how deep I will take you, wench."

Alexi moaned behind the gag and raised her head, wishing she could scream at him to fuck her already. The blindfold kept her from seeing him, but she could smell and feel everything with such clarity that the sensations were nearly driving her out of her mind. Afraid that he was going to torture her more, and withhold his cock from her, she remained completely still.

"Much better, wench." He moved his cock back to the opening of her core, and she whimpered behind the gag. "For a serving girl you have misbehaved far too many times."

Her arms and legs trembled as he gripped her hips and slowly entered her—but then he pulled back until his cock was outside her core again, and this time she almost cried. She was crazy with need for him. Why was he doing this to her?

While she waited for him to torture her more, she breathed in the musky scent of his sweat and testosterone. The calluses on his hands against her hips felt sensual and his warm breath upon her back was like a caress. He moved his cock into the entrance to her core, and she prepared for him to tease her again.

But with a fierce growl, he drove his cock deep into her core.

Alexi screamed behind her gag. It felt so good having him inside her. He was long and thick and hard, and more than anything she'd ever had or even imagined.

"You enjoy this punishment, do you not, wench?" Darronn said as he thrust in and out of her, and the wet sounds of their flesh slapping together filled the room. He smacked her ass cheeks again with his palm and then the strap, and she gave a muffled cry of excitement. "It pleases you to be taken by your lord and Master."

Barely realizing what she was doing, Alexi nodded. *Yes, fuck me, Master. Fuck me!*

"Do not climax yet." Harder and harder he thrust within her core, driving deep, deep inside her. Alexi's orgasm built to such a fierce intensity that she was positive she would explode.

His sweat dripped onto her back, and the smell of her juices and his musky smell were making her crazy.

I'm going to come. I can't hold back any longer.

As if in answer to her thoughts, Darronn roared, "You may climax, wench."

Her body responded so quickly to his permission that it shocked her. Alexi's orgasm blazed through her, burning her belly, her arms, her face. She screamed again behind the gag, as her body jerked and bucked against his, the inferno moving through her like it would never end.

Distantly she heard Darronn's triumphant shout, felt his cock pulsate inside her, and the warm flush of his seed. Her world spun behind her blindfold, and it was like she'd entered a sort of twilight zone. White sparks flying in the darkness, her body like one giant nerve that felt every convulsion of her core, and every throb of his cock.

"A most perfect match," Darronn was saying when he withdrew from her.

She hardly knew what she was doing when she shook her head, begging that he stay inside her. Part of her realized that the motion should have been to deny his statement that they were a perfect match, but right now she didn't care. She just wanted him to screw her again.

All of a sudden she was free, as if he'd used his magic to release her. He immediately pulled her into his lap and he began untying her gag and her blindfold. His cock was definitely hard against her backside, and she wondered how many rounds of good hard sex a Tarok man could handle.

When she could see again, the early morning sunshine pouring into Darronn's chambers caused her to blink and shield her eyes. He didn't give her time to rest. Instead he slipped her off his lap and pushed her onto the bed so that she was flat on her back, looking up at him as he moved between her thighs. And she was still clenching the spade in her fist.

"Wow," she said, her mouth feeling strange and rusty after being gagged for so long. "That was unbelievable."

He gave a sinful smile that she knew would be outlawed in half the U.S. "You have been well punished for your bad behavior, wench."

She licked her lips. "What if I'm thinking about being real bad again, real soon?"

Darronn's smile turned positively untamed. "Then you must be punished at once." And with that he drove into her again.

CHAPTER SEVEN

A TAROK WEEK LATER, ALEXI STOOD ON THE balcony outside the king's chamber, enjoying the panoramic view. She drank in the beauty of Darronn's realm while she waited for him to return to his quarters. Mist rolled off the falls in the waning sunlight, the ever-present roar of the falls her only companionship at this moment.

While she watched Darronn's subjects at work and at play, she grasped the smooth granite wall of the balcony that was only as high as her waist. Often from this vantage point she had seen couples having sex in the forest, or even in the terraced gardens. Heck, sometimes she would see three and four people going at it. No one seemed to care if they were seen screwing away.

Beneath her bare feet the granite flooring was cold and a breeze caressed all the parts of her skin not covered by the leather clothing Darronn had provided. The mountain air was fresh and invigorating, but her nipples were rock hard beneath the straps of leather that criss-crossed her breasts. Her outfit was skimpy, like all the minidresses he'd given her. No, they didn't hide a whole lot, but they sure made her feel sexy as hell.

This past week after her first fabulous fuck with Darronn had flown by incredibly fast. Their days were longer in this world, so she'd actually been in Spades for approximately a week and a half in Earth time, yet it often seemed as if she'd just arrived. She'd been there long enough that Darronn no longer sported a black eye.

It was strange how comfortable she felt in this alien world, and how much she'd come to enjoy every minute she spent with Darronn. But at the same time she desperately missed her aunt Awai and cousin Annie, and hell, she missed her work, her office, and her secretary, Angie. What were they doing now? How were they handling her disappearance? God, she hated the thought of making her friends, family, and coworkers worry by just up and vanishing . . . like Alice had.

Alexi swallowed, but the lump in her throat was about the size of a cannonball as she thought about her twin. She had missed Alice for so long. The ache in her heart would never go away until she found her.

Damn it. I've got to escape and get back to San Francisco, and find Alice!

With a sigh she moved to the wooden trellis and breathed in the rich scent of the purple ravenwood blooms. Their sweet perfume was soothing in the clear spring air, but their countless thorns were a reminder that things weren't always what they seemed. Beautiful and peaceful, yet a real bitch if you got too close.

Careful not to prick herself on a thorn, Alexi plucked a bloom and brought it to her nose and inhaled. It had a thick perfume that reminded her of jasmine. Almost too strong, but she liked it.

In many ways it was hard to believe she was a captive because she was enjoying herself too damn much. Darronn certainly kept her well fed and well pleasured. He had shared with her little of himself, though. She knew that he had three brothers, a niece and nephew, and a sister-in-law, and that his parents had passed away around twenty Tarok years ago. But other than that, he didn't say a whole lot about himself.

Often he took her *jul*-back riding and hiking through the forest, and on picnics beside the waterfall. She wanted to keep in shape, and the hiking had been great exercise. Her lips curved into a grin. Talking about great exercise . . . they'd had sex here and there and everywhere they'd gone. Damn, but that man's appetite matched hers perfectly. He was insatiable.

But Darronn also kept her mostly to himself. She'd gotten to know the servant Kira and the sorceress Kalina a bit, but Darronn rarely left her with the women for long. Not to mention that he rarely left her alone, and when he did he locked her in tight. At night when he went hunting, he not only locked the double doors leading from his room into the rest of the château, but also the balcony doors.

Why did he bother locking those? It was so damn

high . . . Alexi frowned as she took a better look at the trellis and touched the hard wood between a cluster of blooms and the thorny vine. Yeah, it would be easy to climb down it, if you didn't mind a few hundred scratches . . . but where would she go if she did escape?

The dreams.

Alexi set the ravenwood bloom on the low granite wall and it immediately was swept off the balcony by the wind. It swirled and twisted through the air, just like the memory of her nightly visions. Well, at least that's what they seemed like. She'd never had recurring dreams before, but ever since arriving here she'd dreamed that she was in the meadow and the mirror had been there, waiting for her.

Could it possibly be?

She ran her finger over another ravenwood petal. As she withdrew her hand, a thorn pricked her finger. "Damn it," she muttered as she backed away.

And smacked into a solid wall of muscle.

She started to turn around, but Darronn grasped her shoulders and murmured, "Let me see your finger, firecat."

Alexi shivered at his low and vibrant tone and raised the finger where a single drop of blood had collected like a red tear. Darronn leaned over her shoulder and grasped her wrist below her gold bracelet. He brought her finger to his mouth and gently licked the blood away then sucked on her finger.

A moan slipped from Alexi's throat before she could stop it.

"Every part of you tastes as honeyed as the nectar of ravenwood blooms," he whispered by her ear as he pushed her auburn hair over her shoulder.

"You're definitely one hell of a sweet-talker, Your Highness," Alexi replied.

Darronn gave a soft laugh and in the next moment he wrapped one arm around her middle. He placed his free hand at her nape and gently pushed, forcing her to bend over at the waist and putting her off balance. It was a dominant move that placed her completely at his mercy, helpless to do anything.

And it turned her on more than she wanted to admit.

"Hold on to the wall," he said in a low, sensual tone.

Alexi reached out and grabbed the smooth wall as she stared out at his realm. "What if someone sees us?" The thought of being watched as Darronn took her was both unnerving and exciting all at once.

"They will see naught but my hips thrusting against yours, and know only that I claim you."

Quivering with excitement, Alexi gave in to the desire that now set her entire body on fire. She gripped the low wall tighter and widened her stance. "What will you do to me, Master?"

"I wish to see your lovely ass." Darronn removed his arm from around her waist then pushed the skirt of her dress up over her hips. Alexi bit her lip to keep from moaning as he caressed her buttocks. "You have been a well-behaved wench of late."

He still kept his hand on the back of her neck,

keeping her from rising up. She could see the gardeners at work. A man and woman were screwing in the swing that hung from the massive blue feathery leafed *ch'tok* tree in one corner of the tiered gardens. "Will you reward me, Master?" she asked, hoping to hell he would and soon.

"Your skin is pale and beautiful, like a starflower bloom." Darronn stopped caressing her ass. Her heart beat faster as she heard the soft sound of leather lacings being undone and then felt the tip of his cock pressed to her core. "What would you like as your reward, firecat?"

Alexi tried to push back against his cock, but his grip on her neck kept her from moving. "I want you to fuck me, Master."

"Suitable compensation for such a lusty wench." He moved his cock just a fraction inside her pussy and stopped. "What else would you enjoy?"

She didn't hesitate. "To have you pinching one of my nipples while I play with the other one."

"Very good." Darronn kept the one hand at her neck but brought his other to one of her breasts and yanked down on the thin strap. "Fondle your other nipple if you wish for me to take you now."

"Yes, Master." Alexi held on to the balcony wall with one hand and used her other to free her breast. She pulled and tugged on the nipple while Darronn attended to the opposite one.

When Darronn drove into her core, she gasped and

stopped touching herself as she became lost in the sensation of having his cock inside her.

"Play with your breast, wench, or I shall stop."

Immediately Alexi fondled her nipple while he tugged at her other one and took her. Damn but the sensations were so incredible, so unbelievable. She moaned as she watched the servants go about their work, watched people strolling in the gardens, and then again turned her gaze toward the couple screwing in the garden swing. If anyone noticed her and Darronn going at it, they sure weren't making it obvious.

Just as she was close to coming, Darronn stopped and she almost screamed. "You are far too loud, wench," he murmured as he released her neck just long enough to gag her with a silk cloth.

Alexi was glad he had, because she'd been close to screaming and she wasn't sure she wanted everyone to look up at the balcony and see her and Darronn.

He placed one hand on her neck again, the other at her breast, and began taking her with slow, methodical strokes.

Faster! she wanted to scream, but the gag held her cry back. *Harder!*

She was so close, so damn close, but not quite there. But the moment Darronn said, "Come for me, firecat," it was like a match set to a bonfire. Her orgasm roared through her, the flames hot and wild. She screamed behind her gag as he continued plunging in and out of her, drawing her climax out for an eternity.

Moments later Darronn purred as he came, his cock throbbing inside her as he released his semen into her core. How he held back his normal bellow, she didn't know, because she sure as hell couldn't hold back hers.

After Alexi enjoyed a rather erotic bath with the gorgeous hunk of a king, he escorted her to the private dining chambers where a table for two had been set with golden plates, flatware, and goblets bearing the Spades crest. It was now evening and the buttery glow of candles filled the room. Candlelight flickered from the candelabra at the center of the black tablecloth and from several sconces upon the walls.

Like every other place in his château, the room was gorgeous. This one was filled with oil paintings of men and women, and she wondered who they all were.

Once he had seated her at the table to his right, and then had seated himself, servants appeared bearing platters of roasted fowl and roasted vegetables, along with several other delicacies. Kira appeared for only a moment as she poured amber ale into their goblets, and then she quietly slipped out of the room.

Alexi was in a good mood and dug into the meal with enthusiasm. Unlike her sister, Alexi never had to watch her weight. She'd always thought Alice was beautiful just the way she was, but her twin had struggled to accept herself. Since she hadn't had to face what Alice went through, Alexi could only be supportive and had done her best to try to make her twin realize that she really was gorgeous, inside and out.

As usual, thoughts of her missing sister dampened her mood. To turn her mind to something else, she gave a sweeping gesture and asked, "Who are all these people?"

"In the portrait above the fireplace are my parents, the former High King and Queen of Tarok."

He pointed to the one beside it. "That is Jarronn. He and his new queen are now the High King and Queen of Tarok as well as King and Queen of Hearts. Jarronn is my twin, the eldest by several hours."

"I didn't realize he's your twin." Alexi studied the black-haired man in the portrait and noticed the heart tattoo on his biceps. "You're obviously fraternal twins like Alice and me. The two of you don't look anything alike, except for your eyes."

Darronn seemed disinclined to discuss his elder brother, and gestured past his own portrait to one of another dark-haired man with penetrating black eyes. He was bare chested and positioned in a side view so that the diamond tattoo at the back of his right shoulder was visible. "My younger brother Karn, King of Diamonds." And then he pointed out a blond man with a club tattoo and a devilish smile. "The youngest, Ty, is King of Clubs."

Alexi's eyes moved to the portrait of a blond woman who had a captivating smile, although something about her eyes seemed dark. "Who is she?" Alexi asked when Darronn didn't volunteer the information.

Darronn gave a casual shrug. "The youngest of the Tarok clan." His voice grew soft as he said, "The portrait was done a long time ago, before the sister I knew and loved died."

"I'm sorry, Darronn."

He shook his head. "Do not be. It was of her own doing."

Suicide? Alexi wondered, but she did not ask aloud. It was obvious from the look in his expressive green eyes that he did not want to discuss his sister, so she changed the subject. "My cousin Annie is an artist, but she primarily does landscapes." Alexi frowned at the thought of her cousin, who would be worried sick by now.

Darronn actually smiled as he glanced back to the picture of the former High King and Queen of Tarok. "My mother was the artist who painted all that you see. Even the one of her and my father."

Alexi smiled as she admired the paintings. "She was incredibly talented."

When they finished eating, and Alexi had downed a good two goblets of ale and was feeling fiiiiiiine, Kira appeared with a platter of strawberry tarts. Alexi glanced up at the picture of the King of Hearts and almost sniggered. Was Darronn the knave who stole the King and Queen of Hearts' tarts?

While they each ate their share of tarts, Darronn asked her questions about her life and her career in San Francisco. He seemed particularly interested in her law practice. "In Spades we have need of a new arbitrator. . . ." He broke off and leaned forward, his green eyes focused on her. "What happened, firecat, to make you so distrustful of men?"

His question caused her strawberry tart to stick in her throat. She grasped her goblet and swallowed a large gulp of the smooth ale. After all the ale she'd had, she felt loose and relaxed enough to talk with him about one of the worst times in her life. When she set the goblet back onto the black tablecloth, her gaze met his.

"During my last year of law school, I started dating a guy from one of my classes. His name was Larry." She dabbed her lips with a napkin. "He was intelligent and gorgeous, not to mention the sex we had together was great." She almost laughed at the scowl that darkened Darronn's handsome face. But then she frowned, too, as she thought back to those days when she'd been so naïve. "I really thought he was perfect for me. And I thought I'd fallen in love."

"What did he do to you?" Darronn asked through clenched teeth. "If the bastard harmed you I will track him down and kill him."

Alexi almost smiled again at Darronn's protectiveness. "Larry didn't harm me. At least not physically." She turned her gaze to the goblet and trailed her fingers up and down the slender shaft as she became lost in her thoughts.

"He used me," she said. "I was the top student in law school and he was second only to me. I later found out that he had been taking my class work and copying it." Anger and hurt swelled up within her at the memories. "I was so stupid. It wasn't until we were close to graduation that I found out. One of my papers had vanished. I discovered that Larry had turned it in as his own."

The fury that struck her at the memory was almost surprising in its intensity. "I talked to the professor, but he sided with Larry, who claimed that I had stolen it from him. Seems the old boys' club didn't like a woman being valedictorian."

She gripped the goblet's stem so tight it was a wonder it didn't crumple in her hand. "When I confronted Larry about it, he just laughed and said he'd been using me all along. That I'd better learn quick not to be so damn trusting if I was going to make it in law."

The corner of her mouth quirked in a wry smile as her gaze met Darronn's furious green gaze. "I thanked Larry for the lesson and then taught him to guard his nuts."

Darronn winced.

"Yeah, that bastard was walking and talking funny for about a week." Alexi picked up her goblet. "You should feel lucky. I blackened both his eyes, broke his nose, and rammed his balls up his throat."

The king snorted and Alexi could tell he wasn't sure how to react. Whether to be pissed at the asshole who had hurt her, or to laugh at her revenge on him.

"Larry taught me a lesson all right, and so did the class professor." Alexi swirled the ale in her goblet. "I showed both of them, though. I aced absolutely every final exam and wrote an award-winning paper that more than replaced the one Larry stole from me. But I've never trusted a man since."

Darronn reached out and placed his palm on top of her free hand. "I would never hurt you intentionally, firecat. Know that you can trust in me. I do what I believe is best for you as well as for my subjects."

Alexi tipped her head back and downed the last of her ale. She thunked it onto the tablecloth and gave him a direct look. "I've heard that one before, Darronn. I trust no one but myself, my sister, and my aunt and cousin. I don't trust my scum of a father who ran off with some bimbo and left me and Alice. And I can't trust my mom because she's been gone mentally for a very long time."

She tried to pull her hand away from Darronn, but he wouldn't let go. "Trust me," he said, his words intense and fierce, like a command.

Slowly she shook her head. "Trust is earned. Not given."

CHAPTER EIGHT

THREE MORE WEEKS PASSED BEFORE ALEXI FInally found the opportunity to make her escape. She woke in Darronn's bed knowing that now was her chance. It was dark in the bedroom, with only a sliver of moonlight slipping through a gap in the draperies—and Darronn wasn't in bed with her. No doubt he was out prowling the forest behind the château, something he did most nights. She hated that she missed him when he wasn't in bed with her, and it was time to make those feelings go away.

She crawled out of bed and hurried to the balcony doors. With one tug they opened. Just like in her dream.

Alexi hurried to her trunk to put on some clothing. She'd been in Spades for almost two Earth months. Long enough that she no longer missed her morning caffeine ritual. The morning ritual of having great sex with Darronn had been far more stimulating . . . and she would definitely miss him. Or rather, the sex.

Yeah, that's it. The sex.

Hell, who was she kidding? She'd miss the big oaf, too.

But it's time to get back to San Francisco and find my sister.

Over the past weeks they'd played a variety of sexual games, with him always dominating her. It was exciting to let him command her—but in bed only. And the fact that he stuck with his promise and didn't try to dominate her in front of anyone else meant a lot to her.

Alexi found a leather outfit that didn't expose her quite as much as the others did, and tugged it on as her thoughts continued to center on Darronn. During the day he took her with him most places he went, whether it was around the château to speak with servants, or into the village to meet with his subjects. It was obvious in all his dealings that he was good to his people, listening to them, ensuring their needs were met. He was fair in all that she'd witnessed since she'd arrived in Spades. She admired him, and he made her feel somehow alive and vibrant, and almost happy.

Almost, because she needed to find Alice before she could truly be happy again. Besides, she knew better than to trust men.

It's time to leave.

Every single night for about a Tarok month she'd had the same dream where she was in the meadow, standing before the mirror. But tonight was the first night she'd actually seen herself slip out of the château, onto the balcony, down the trellis, through the terraced gardens, then into the village. Her dream had taken her all the way through the village, the forest, and finally to the meadow.

And tonight was the first time she had seen her cousin and aunt in the dream.

After Alexi had slipped on the dress, she quickly braided her hair into a single plait to keep it out of her face, and tied the end of the braid with one of the leather straps that Darronn had left at their bedside. While she fixed her hair, she turned the dream over and over in her mind. She had seen the mirror right where it had been when he captured her and brought her to Tarok. Through its surface she could see her town house, still in immaculate condition.

But this time her cousin Annie had been leaning against the door frame of the bedroom, a sad look in her eyes. It had been an even bigger surprise when Aunt Awai slipped by Annie and into the bedroom. Awai's slim form had been clothed in a tight leather minidress, and she'd been wearing boots that reached her thighs—and Alexi could swear her aunt was carrying a whip in one hand. Talk about an unusual dream—Awai wore only tailored business suits to work, and when not at her job she always wore expensive and chic slacks and sweaters.

In her dream, Alexi couldn't hear what Awai and Annie were saying to each other. But when Annie had gestured to the carpet, Alexi had seen the can of Mace right where she'd dropped it. She'd even seen the indentations from her stilettos that led through the plush carpet and straight toward where the mirror had been.

Or where it is right this minute. She was certain it was there.

When Alexi finished with her hair, she hurried to the balcony doors. Her heart beat faster as she slipped through the opening, into the moonlit night. She quietly shut them after her, forcing herself not to look back, as she left Darronn and his world behind.

With the doors being unlocked, just like in her dream, Alexi knew the vision of her escape had been an omen. Darronn never forgot to lock her in, and she didn't think it was a coincidence that he had forgotten tonight. Even though he treated her with respect and caring, he'd known she would attempt an escape, and he was always careful to check the locks.

Of course the old Alexi would think the new Alexi was nuts. But since she'd been in Tarok she'd seen enough crazy things to make her a believer of just about anything.

The granite balcony floor was cold beneath her bare feet as she hurried to the trellis, and she wished she had shoes. But her red stilettos just weren't going to cut it for making a quick getaway, and her hiking shoes were always left at the back entrance of the château. Probably to keep her from attempting this very thing and escaping.

Ravenwood thorns pricked at her flesh the moment she climbed onto the solid wood of the trellis. The normally purple blooms were an odd shimmering black in the moonlight, and their scent was thick and ominous rather than soothing like normal. With every step down, thorns scraped against the bared flesh that her skimpy leather outfit didn't cover. They abraded her belly, the exposed parts of her breasts, her shoulders, her face, her legs, her feet. Blood soon trickled from several of the wounds and they itched like mad.

Her fight against the thorns along with her struggle to reach the bottom of the trellis without falling and killing herself kept her mind occupied. And then, when she finally felt soft grass beneath her feet, she turned and fled into the terraced gardens.

Alexi concentrated on avoiding guards and blending in with the shadows. She was determined. She wouldn't fail.

The night smelled of damp forest and of the strong scent of the ravenwood blooms still clinging to her skin and clothing. Above the sound of the thundering falls, a wolf's distant howl caused her to shiver. What if there were predators out here . . . other than Darronn?

She shoved away all thoughts of him, refusing to dwell on them. Instead she focused on traveling as silently as possible. Soon her feet felt frozen in addition to being cut and bruised from the flower trellis and from sticks and small rocks poking out of the forest loam. Through the trees warm light from the village beckoned her. Thank goodness this portion of the forest wasn't too thick or she'd never have been able to find her way in the dark.

When she was far enough away from the château to feel a little safer, she couldn't keep her thoughts and feelings back any longer.

It was actually tearing at her heart and soul to leave Darronn.

Damn it!

How could she have allowed the man to get so completely under her skin the way he had? With Darronn she'd had the best sex of her life, every day for the past few Tarok weeks. Several times a day, in fact. But more than that, he touched a chord within her. It still amazed her that such a powerful, imposing man had cared enough to compromise in order to please her.

In public they had visibly shocked his people because she walked at his side and kept her head held high. It was apparently even more shocking that she did not wear his collar of ownership or the nipple piercings that she learned were expected of his personal attendants and of his future queen. She had often sensed that it both confused and intrigued his servants and subjects, but they respected their king enough not to question his wisdom or his decisions.

When she had talked to Darronn about her missing sister, he had promised that she would see Alice again, and she believed that he had every intention of helping her. But she couldn't wait around for him to decide the time was right. She had to find her twin *now*.

It was chilly enough that the blue-green mist began to rise up from the ground, reminding her of the day she'd woken strapped and bound to golden stakes in the meadow. Moonlight glinted off her bracelets as it seeped through the trees.

Once Alexi slipped into the village, she passed as close to several cottages as she dared, hoping to find some kind of shoes. By the time she'd reached the other end of the village, she'd just about given up hope when she spotted some. Beside a cottage door was a pair of boots that looked a little big, but close enough to her size to fit.

She hurried over to the house, moving as quietly as possible. But as she reached for the boots, it occurred to her that they could be a child's shoes, and what if the family was too poor to afford more?

Shaking her head, Alexi slowly straightened and then backed away. Sighing, she flipped her braid over her shoulder and ran her fingers through her loose bangs. She'd rather have her feet freeze off than steal from someone who needed shoes more than she did.

Skin along her spine crawled and hair prickled at her nape. Something—or someone—was watching her.

Darronn crouched, ready to pounce on the *anlia* buck, when he scented a change in the wind. The buck apparently sensed it, too, and bolted into the forest.

Holding back a growl, Darronn raised his muzzle. Alexi's sweet musk teased his nose, and then the smell of her blood nearly drove him into a rage. Had she been abducted from his room? The bastard would be dead before he made it beyond the village.

He bounded through the forest, toward his woman,

scenting the wind as he ran. He caught no unusual smells, only Alexi's fragrance of starflower and midnight mingling with the familiar night perfume of his realm.

Alexi was attempting to leave him.

The realization tore at his gut and his heart as he sped toward his mate. After all they had shared during her time in Spades, Darronn had hoped she would feel something for him, as he did for her.

Holding back a roar of anger and frustration, he bounded over streams and logs, through bushes and around boulders. He had been hunting a good distance from his château, and was far yet from his woman. Dangers still abounded in his realm. If she stumbled upon a rogue mountain wolf, a river bear, or a cave-dwelling primitive . . . Darronn growled and doubled his speed.

Thank the skies Mikaela's attention remained on Hearts these days. Her mind-war had affected Darronn's people, as it had all of Tarok, but since the battle of last summer no mindspells had been cast in Spades. In this the sorceress Kalina had been certain.

Every day Darronn had shared with his future queen had made him desire and respect her more. Alexi was beautiful, fiery, intelligent, stubborn, and determined. It amazed him how easily he had given in to compromise with his mate, and how much it pleased him to have a woman with such inner strength.

She spoke often of her sister, Alice, and Darronn knew that one day he would need to inform her that her sister was indeed safe and well, and that she was now the High Queen of Tarok. Of course one day he would take

Alexi to see her sister, but he knew that first his mate needed to find her place in this world, at his side. And her soul still needed to heal.

Although she gave willingly of her body, she had given him nothing of her heart. He ached to know more of her, but she kept much of her feelings sealed tight inside where not even the strongest of wills could unlock them and set them free.

While he ran toward his mate, it occurred to Darronn that Alexi gave no more than she received. He had shared with her very little of his past, of his disappointments and failures, or even his triumphs. If he opened more to her, would she in turn open to him?

The fact that he was even considering such a thing would have been enough to give him pause if he'd had the time to spare.

When he neared the village Alexi's perfume grew stronger, and Darronn slowed his pace to a steady lope. He scented no dangers around her. She was alone, and he was certain she was making her way back toward the meadow where he had taken her. Likely in hopes the looking glass would be there.

His fear for his woman turned to anger that flamed in his gut. Alexi's defection dishonored him. If his people knew she had left him, they would begin to doubt his ability to perform his duties as King of Spades.

At the end of the village her scent was so strong it would have driven him to his knees were he in his man form. He slowly stalked his prey, stopping in the shadows of a cottage when he saw her.

She was looking at a pair of shoes beside a doorstep. Blood trickled down countless cuts upon her legs, arms, face. It was obvious she had climbed down the trellis to the terraced gardens. When he returned with her to the château, he would ensure the immediate removal of the trellis.

He watched as she reached for the boots and he narrowed his gaze. Would she take from his people, only to serve her immediate need?

But Alexi shook her head, straightened her posture, then backed away. He had sensed the war within her and her final decision, which pleased him greatly. Yet it did nothing to dispel his anger at her for leaving him.

Alexi went still and fear flashed across her face, and he knew she had sensed his presence.

Heart pounding, Alexi slipped into the shadows behind the cottage and hurried out of the village. When she reached the forest path, she ran. Chill air rushed over her bared skin as she bolted through the trees. The moonlit path was bright enough to allow her to run without tripping, but the forest was growing denser, the mist thicker, and soon she would be forced to walk—if her bare feet didn't freeze first.

A snapping sound echoed through the forest behind her. Alexi's heart went into overdrive and she increased her speed. Her lungs ached, her mouth tasted like copper, and blood rushed in her head.

Something was after her.

What can I do?

Climb a tree! She bolted off the dirt path and into the thick forest grass, but it was so dark she could barely see and she had to slow down. Alexi sized up tree after tree, but those big enough to climb were all too tall for her—no branches low enough for her to grab onto.

She stumbled over a root and dropped to her hands and knees. Rocks and twigs dug into her flesh and stung at the wounds from the trellis. She forced herself up again, frantically searching for a tree to hide in.

There!

A yard, maybe two yards ahead. Her feet ached and her body burned from all the scratches, and her lungs felt like they would burst. She reached the tree and grabbed the lowest branch to pull herself up.

Something slammed into her back. Alexi screamed and lost her grip on the branch. She pitched forward and landed facefirst in a pile of leaves and dirt. Air whooshed from her lungs, and when she sucked her breath in, her mouth filled with debris. Her head spun with fear as a mammoth creature pinned her to the ground, its paws braced against the skin left bare by her skimpy dress. Her cuts and scrapes burned and she was having problems catching her breath.

But what did that matter if she was about to be eaten?

The beast's tremendous roar shattered the night.

Darronn. She would know his roar anywhere, and if she hadn't been so scared, she would have recognized his primal scent right away, too.

Relief followed by a quick dose of fear washed over

her in warm then cold waves. She was glad it was Darronn who had her pinned and not some other beast—but from the tone of his roar, he was good and pissed at her.

But he wouldn't hurt her . . . would he?

Wait a minute. She shouldn't be relieved it was him. She should be angry that he had screwed up her escape plan.

It is obvious I have been far too lenient with you, the king's voice growled in her mind. *I intend to remedy that at once.*

Alexi spat dirt and leaves from her mouth and tried to get up, but he had her pinned too tightly. "Goddammit, Darronn. What did you expect? You kidnap me and I'm supposed to just go with it? Now get off!"

You wish me to apologize? Choosing and claiming is the way of our people! Darronn's claws flexed, pricking her flesh, but not too deeply. *I honor you by my choice, I offer you my kingdom, my companionship, my—and you dishonor me?*

"I'm no one's captive." She sniffed, feeling uncertain. "Not even yours."

Silence, wench! he shouted in her mind.

"Screw you." Alexi struggled to get out from under his tiger paws. "You overgrown, hairy, big-dicked son of a bitch!"

Darronn roared again, and leaves literally showered down from the trees and landed on Alexi's head.

His weight shifted . . . and the paws on her bare back turned into his hands. In the next moment Darronn was forcing her legs apart and kneeling between her thighs. "I can make you beg for my cock," he said, as he kept her pinned with one hand around her neck and yanked her dress up with his other. "I could have ensured long ago that you would have no desire to leave me."

"Like hell." Alexi bit back a moan as he pressed his leather-clad erection to her bare ass and ground her pussy against the bed of leaves beneath her. Her breasts felt swollen and needy, and her clit ached like mad. "All I ever wanted from you was a good lay. It's time to move on."

"No more lies. No more games. You are captive to your own refusal to love." With a fierce growl, Darronn leaned over her back and bit her shoulder, causing her to gasp out loud as he marked her again. At the same time a heavy musk surrounded Alexi, and it seemed to come from him. She stiffened as her body absorbed the musk, which filled her senses and blurred her thoughts.

All of a sudden she was wild with lust and raging warmth filled her body, chasing away the chill and even making her feet warm. Her mind became so clouded with passion and desire that she could think of nothing but screwing Darronn. She needed him so badly she couldn't stand another moment without his cock inside her.

Alexi thrashed against him, arching her ass tighter against his erection while trying to break free of his grip. "Please, Darronn. Now!"

"How must you refer to me, wench?" he asked as he moved his hips away from hers, denying her even the pleasure of his cock against her skin.

"Master." Alexi's body was shaking so badly for him, her mind so filled with desire, that she could think of nothing but what it would take to please him. "Fuck me, Master."

Darronn backed away. She scrambled to her knees and practically lunged at him. He grabbed her braid, forcing her to remain on her knees. His features were stern and masterful, his eyes unforgiving as he looked at her. "You will do as I say or I will not give you the plea-sure of my cock inside your quim. It is time you under-stood that sometimes, someone other than Alexi might know best."

Alexi whimpered, but waited for his instructions, knowing that she was going to go out of her mind if he didn't take her soon. Somewhere in the back of her mind she knew this was crazy—why was she acting this way? But the lust was so intense she didn't give a damn. She had to have him.

Using his free hand, Darronn yanked down the strips of leather covering her breasts, exposing them to his gaze and the chill air of the forest. He then waved his hand and his clothing vanished completely, as he'd done many times in their bedroom.

When had she started to think of it as *their* bed-room?

His grip on her hair remained tight as he drew her toward his hips. "Suck my cock, wench."

Without hesitation, Alexi took him into her mouth and wrapped her fingers around the base of his shaft. God, but she loved to go down on him. Okay, so she might have been running away, but it wasn't because she didn't like being with this hunk of a kidnapping bastard.

She squirmed as he held her braid tighter and took control of her movements, thrusting his cock in and out. She always enjoyed sucking him off, but right now she wanted him in her instead. Damn, but she needed to come.

He never allowed it when he mastered her in the bedroom, but she had to get herself off now. She moved one of her hands to her slit, into her drenched folds, and bucked her hips against her fingers in time with the movements of his cock into her mouth.

Abruptly he stopped his thrusts. "You have added yet another punishment to your list," Darronn said as he removed his erection from her mouth. In a movement so fast her head spun, he took her hand from his cock and her other from her clit. "I have not given you permission to pleasure yourself."

"I need to come, Master." Alexi didn't understand why she was so easily slipping into the subservient role she always played in their bedroom, but at this moment she was beyond thinking. "Please!"

Even as she begged, he moved behind her and bound her wrists behind her back by fastening her bracelets together with his magic. More of the exciting musk scent emanated from him and her pussy became so wet that her thighs were slick with moisture. Her entire body quivered with desire and she knew she'd just die if he didn't take her soon.

Alexi yelped as he grabbed her by the waist and flipped her around. He flung her over his shoulder and marched deeper into the dark forest.

CHAPTER NINE

BLOOD RUSHED TO ALEXI'S HEAD WHEN DARronn tossed her over his shoulder and her braid flipped into her eyes. The tie slipped off the end and fell to the forest floor.

Like Hansel and Gretel, it marks our path, she thought, and would have laughed if she didn't need Darronn so badly.

Her body burned from her many wounds. While he carried her through the forest, branches scraped her naked ass since her dress was up around her waist. Her now bared nipples rubbed against his back as she watched the flex of his bare ass cheeks. She could picture his buttocks flexing and tensing as he drove into her again and again, and she moaned and thrashed against him. "I can't take any more, Master. Please."

"Quiet, wench." He slapped her ass with his palm, and the sting brought tears to her eyes and warm pleasure to her folds. He kept one arm tight around her legs, but at the same time he used his free hand to spread her legs a little.

A gasp escaped her throat as he pushed something thick and rubbery between her thighs and up inside her. She was sure it was the spade vibrator that she loved so much, the one he frequently enjoyed using on her. "Do not climax without permission," he ordered.

She cried out as the thing began to vibrate inside her. Alexi pumped her hips against his shoulder, trying to bring herself closer to what she needed so badly, even though she knew that just an orgasm wouldn't solve the fierce demand her body had for Darronn. She needed *him* inside her, needed him to complete her.

The vibrations stopped and Darronn swatted her ass again. "You know the rules." He withdrew the spade vibrator from her core, and she almost sobbed. He was trying to drive her crazy, she just knew it.

"Why are you doing this to me?" Alexi's breathing was so heavy now she could barely speak. "Why won't you take me?"

"You must be taught a lesson." Darronn ducked, and from her upside down position she realized they had just entered a cave. It was dark at first, but soon a dim orange glow made it light enough for her to see as he continued to walk. His boot steps sounded loud and threatening in the semidarkness.

"I won't leave again." Alexi couldn't believe the words were coming out of her mouth, but she couldn't stop them. "I need you inside me, Master."

A deep scraping sound rumbled through the cave, followed by a rush of cool, moist air that tightened her nipples. The air smelled somehow woodsy, yet musty, too. Darronn stepped through the entrance and she saw a stone door sliding down behind them, and heard its ominous slam when it sealed itself shut.

He slid her from his shoulders and her dress fell back down around her hips. Grasping her by the shoulders, he turned her to face the room, and she caught her breath.

A small waterfall, more like a fountain of rocks, spilled into a small pool in one corner of a medium-sized semidark cavern. Amethyst and black crystals sparkled along the walls and ceiling and reflected off the waterfall and the pool. It was like being in an amazingly cool nature-made discothèque lit with sparkling purple crystals instead of a black light and a disco ball.

As she studied the cavern in openmouthed wonder, Alexi realized there were several naked men and women. Watching her and Darronn.

For a moment Alexi felt like she was in some kind of weird sci-fi movie, the way the cavern glittered and with the naked people observing them.

"I see you have brought me a gift, King Darronn," a gorgeous man said as he broke away from the naked group. Behind him stood five beautiful women with fabulous bodies and two stunning men who were just as hot and sexy as the one crossing the cavern toward Alexi and Darronn.

Alexi could only stare at the man, who was so good-looking he could have been a Greek god. Rippling muscles, rock-hard abs, smooth and tanned skin, and long golden-blond hair. And talk about well hung.

"Lord Kir." Darronn gave a low growl but said nothing else as the god neared them.

Without even realizing at first what she was doing, Alexi moved closer to Darronn, but he stepped behind her, as if distancing himself. The sharp ache that bit into her heart took her by surprise. Why wasn't he keeping her close to him? She felt strangely empty and alone without the possessiveness she'd become accustomed to from him . . . and she realized then that in truth, she enjoyed his possessiveness.

When the god reached them, he ignored Darronn and stared down at Alexi. "I am Lord Kir and would be pleased to serve you, Milady." His vivid blue gaze was carnal and demanding, as if he intended to have her any way he chose. Before Alexi could react, the god took her hand, raised it to his mouth, and kissed her knuckles. His lips were warm and sensuous, and he flicked his tongue against her skin in a light swipe, like a dog might—or a wolf.

Her body reacted instantly—her nipples tightening and a tingle zinging through her. Alexi frowned and snatched her hand away. It occurred to her that she no longer felt that same intense lust she'd felt with Darronn just moments ago, and she now could think clearly again.

Her desire for Darronn—that hadn't waned. She wanted him just as badly.

"Do you mind telling me what's going on?" Alexi's gaze darted over her shoulder to Darronn, who was just as naked as the blond god, but whose features had hardened into a stone mask. His eyes, though—they held a mixture of emotion she couldn't identify. Fury? Hurt? Something deeper?

"You wish to be fucked." Darronn's tone was even, but she caught a tinge of anger to it. "I am but a convenient cock to fill your quim. Perhaps you would better enjoy Kir, lord of the cave-dwelling mountain wolves?"

Alexi's jaw dropped. She couldn't believe what Darronn was saying. "You would just give me to this—this *man*?"

"Werewolf." Kir leaned close enough for her to feel his body heat and smell his woodsy scent. He loudly sniffed her hair, his cock close enough to brush the leather of her dress. "I could take you with me to Emerald City and pleasure you in ways that would leave you begging for more."

"I don't *think* so." Alexi turned her glare on Kir, placed her hands on his solidly muscled chest, and shoved. Or at least she tried. All she managed to do was get him to stop sniffing her hair. "If you don't want to lose your balls, wolf-boy, you'd better back off."

Kir raised an eyebrow and the corner of his mouth quirked as he straightened. "Do you not wish to have a cock that would please you?" He gestured toward the other two gorgeous males in the room who both stared at her with equally predatory expressions. "Mayhap two or three cocks at once?"

"No." Alexi held her ground and said to him in her man-eating-attorney tone, "If any one of you tries to touch me, I'll ram your balls up your throat and you'll be howling in soprano come full moon."

"Then what *do* you want?" Kir's eyes sparked fire. "Is this a game you play? Is it 'force' you are looking for?" He reached up and trailed his finger down her upper arm. "Or perhaps you desire . . . seduction?"

Alexi knocked his hand away and practically growled at him—as if Darronn's tigerness had rubbed off on her or something. "Let's get this through your pretty golden head, Lord of the Lobos." She pointed her finger at his chest and punctuated each word as she said, "The only big-cocked guy who's going to come near me is Darronn. Got that?"

"Why?" Kir's question was so direct, so simple, it totally caught her off guard.

"Because . . ." Alexi glared at the blue-eyed son of a bitch as she fought to identify the emotions raging through her.

She thought she had never run away from anything in her life, that she faced everything head-on. But suddenly it was all so clear—like finding that last piece of evidence that would ensure she would win a particularly difficult legal case.

Tonight she hadn't just been running away from Darronn to go home and to search for her sister . . . she'd been running away from her feelings for Darronn.

"Yes?" Kir's expression was amused, and she wanted to slug him.

"Damn it." Alexi raised both clenched fists and started beating on the wolf king's bicep like a punching bag. "No way in hell is anyone else going to touch me, because I'm in love with Darronn."

Kir caught her wrists, trapping them in his strong grip and stopping her from hitting him. He bowed and gave a solemn smile. "It is as I had expected. I have no desire to claim a female whose heart belongs to another."

With that he released her. He whirled and shifted into a golden wolf in such a blur she barely saw him transform. The other men and women in the cave shifted, too, and in moments the pack loped across the expansive cavern and through a dark tunnel at the far end.

A haunting howl echoed through the cavern. . . . And then there was nothing but an aching silence punctuated by the light slap of water from the small waterfall, and the beating of Alexi's heart in her ears.

Amethyst and black crystals sparkled around the room and reflected off the waterfall and the small pool of water, making her feel even more like she was in a fantasyland. The woodsy scent in the room had dimmed with the departure of the wolves, leaving the smell of fresh water and Darronn's primal male scent.

She felt his presence behind her, his warmth and strength, even though he wasn't touching her. Crazy emotions spun through her heart, soul, and body. Relief at admitting what she'd been denying all along. Giddiness at truly being in love for the first time in her life. Frustration that it had to be here and now, in this world and not her own, when she had family she'd left behind, and a sister she needed to search for.

She didn't know how and when and where it had happened, at this moment the only thing that mattered was the man behind her.

Taking a deep breath, Alexi slowly turned to see Darronn with his arms folded across his broad chest and a smug look on his handsome face.

Alexi glared at him. "Bastard," she said.

And then she jumped him.

Darronn smiled as he caught her to his chest. "Wench."

She wrapped her arms around his neck, her legs around his waist, and she kissed him with everything she had.

Yeah, she loved the big oaf. Loved the way he commanded her, and the way he made her look at herself instead of trying to run the world. She loved the way he was so good to his people, making sure their needs were met, and the way he was fair and just in everything she'd witnessed since arriving in Spades.

She loved how he had made compromises with her. Allowing her to be her strong, confident self outside the bedroom and not trying to break her when he recognized her need to be who she was. And inside their bedroom, she loved how he dominated her, fulfilling every one of her fantasies.

Darronn growled with satisfaction as his mate thrust her tongue into his mouth, and as he returned her demanding kiss. When she had wrapped her legs around his waist, her dress had eased up to her waist, exposing the folds of her quim, and his cock pressed against her. He wanted to back her up against the cavern wall and drive into her with all that he possessed.

In his many years, never had he dreamed that having his mate declare her love for him would make him feel such emotion. As though he was the most powerful of men, and certainly the most blessed in every way that a man could be.

Alexi pulled away and looked up at Darronn, her eyes dark with passion, her mouth moist and reddened from his stubble. "Do that thing you did to me before," she said, her voice husky with need. "Where you made me crazy for you."

"Are you not crazy for me without the *tigri* pheromones?" he teased.

"Yeah, I am." She anchored her legs tighter around his waist. "But that *tigri* stuff was wild. I want you to take me when I'm like that."

The lust raging through Darronn was so fierce he wasn't sure he could wait to claim her the way he wanted to.

"You must be punished, wench," he said as he forcibly removed her, and set her on her feet.

Alexi's eyes sparked with pleasure as they always did when he dominated her in the bedroom. Her voice had an excited and breathless quality to it when she spoke. "Yes, Master."

When she was standing, he lifted the bottom of her dress and pulled it up over her head in a quick movement and tossed it aside. She started to reach for him, but he held up one hand indicating she should stop.

"Stand in the position of respect," he ordered, and she complied by clasping her hands behind her back and widening her stance. In their bedroom she had enjoyed submitting to him in all ways, although he never insisted she lower her eyes—he enjoyed gazing into their aqua depths too much to have her look away from him.

Not that she would lower her gaze even if he had asked.

But now that she had declared her love, would she wear his signs of ownership—at least when they were alone?

Darronn held out his palm and a black leather collar with gold spades appeared upon it. "My collar, firecat. Will you wear it?"

Alexi's eyes widened, and for once she looked uncertain, but for only a moment. "Yes, Master."

The pleasure at her acceptance was so intense that Darronn's already raging cock thrust out toward her like a mast on a sailing ship. A hint of a smile curved the corner of Alexi's mouth, telling him that she had noticed.

Taking care to barely brush his body against hers, to tease her passions even more, he slowly moved behind her. "Raise your hair, firecat."

She did as he bade, her form trembling with excitement, and the smell of her desire nearly sent Darronn over the edge. He eased the collar around her neck and fastened it. When he finished, he leaned just close enough that his cock touched the small of her back, and he brushed his lips across her nape and kissed the soft skin above her collar.

"You are the fire in my veins," he murmured. "The flames in my soul."

Alexi shivered and let her hair fall as Darronn stepped away. The collar felt comfortable around her neck, and somehow made her hornier yet. Although a part of her couldn't believe she had just allowed him to put his collar on her. What if it was permanent, and never came off? Strangely enough, the idea didn't upset her. At this moment she wanted to be his in every way.

Yet he had never told her how he felt about her, other than stating that she was his destined mate. Would he return her love? And if he did, what next?

She let the thoughts slide away as her man moved around to face her again. Every slight touch of his hands and fingers set her senses on fire. Good Lord, he was a handsome man, so powerful and virile . . . and he was all hers.

Darronn held out his hand again, and this time a pair of golden spades appeared on his palm, each spade on the end of a small loop. Earrings?

"Your nipples are not yet pierced," Darronn said, and Alexi flinched at the thought of anyone sticking a needle through *that* part of her body. And what did he mean, *yet*? "For now will you wear these nipple rings?" he asked.

Well, if this was just play, it did turn her on thinking about it. When she'd seen the servants in the château

141

wearing them, it had always made her wet. "Yes, Master," she whispered, and wondered if she'd lost her mind.

But at the extreme satisfaction in Darronn's gaze, it was all she could do not to squeeze her thighs together. When he lowered his head and laved one nipple, she thought she was going to come unglued. A moan escaped her when Darronn forced the snug ring over her nipple. The slight pressure was delicious, as was the cool gold spade dangling against her breast. Everything about what he was doing felt so good, she was certain she was going to come.

By the time he had fastened both nipple rings on her, Alexi was so hot for him she wasn't sure she could take much more.

"Come, firecat." He took her hand and led her to one of the sparkling amethyst and black walls. The collar felt snug and exciting around her neck, and the spades swinging against her breasts made her want to scream with the need for release. "Lean forward and brace your hands against the wall," he ordered, "and widen your thighs."

Alexi obeyed, planting her feet wide apart and leaning over to place her palms flat against the faceted wall, the spades dangling from her nipples. She loved how it felt, bent over and exposed to Darronn the way she was. It amazed her how completely she trusted him . . . like no man ever before.

She gasped as he slid the familiar black spade vibrator inside her and he murmured, "Remember, firecat, you may not reach climax without permission."

The anticipation of wondering what he was going to do to her this time was driving her wild, but she managed to reply, "Yes, Master."

Alexi moaned as the spade began pulsing in her core in a manner that was different from how she'd experienced it before. It felt so fabulous she had no idea how she was going to keep from coming before he said she could. Darronn must have used magic to keep it inside her because he was now massaging and caressing her butt cheeks with his hands as the vibrator continued to throb in her pussy.

"Such a fine ass." He moved his hips next to hers and she fought to keep from thrusting back against him, knowing that he would deny her if she did. She had to let him control her. "Would you like me to take you?" he asked, the rough timbre of his voice sending more thrills through her.

"Yes, Master." Alexi moaned. "Take me now, please."

"Ah, but you have earned many punishments." Darronn backed away then slid a strap over her back that he had obviously retrieved with his magic.

The caress of leather against her skin made her shiver with anticipation and her heart beat faster, knowing what would come next. "I've been such a bad girl, Master."

"Indeed."

The first lash fell across her buttocks and the vibration of the spade inside her increased. Even the spades at her nipples and the charm at her navel swung faster and almost seemed to hum. Her skin stung then tingled, and then he lashed her again, causing more flames to lick through her body. The bite of each lash quickly turned into fissions of pleasure until she felt she would literally burst into a bonfire of ecstasy.

"May I come, Master?" she whispered when she was almost too close to the edge to pull back.

"No." His sharp command brought her back, just barely. He stopped the lashes and withdrew the spade.

For a moment he just left her there, waiting for him. Not touching her, not speaking. Then she caught the whiff of that incredible musk, that scent he'd called *tigri* pheromones.

Her entire body began to tremble with such force she knew she'd fly apart if she didn't have him now. To hell with waiting, she was just going to turn around . . . but then from behind her, he murmured, "Free yourself. Be wild, firecat."

Alexi pushed away from the wall, spun around, and flung herself at Darronn. She held on with one arm around his neck while she wrapped her legs around his waist. With her free hand she grasped his cock and placed it at the entrance of her core.

Darronn stopped her, holding her by her waist and keeping her from slamming herself down on his cock. She fought him, needing him inside her more than anything in the world. His musk lightened, slightly, but enough that she stilled when she saw the way that he was looking at her.

Lust, passion, and she was certain she saw love in his green eyes, too.

His mouth came down hard on hers at the same time the *tigri* musk became stronger and he brought her down hard, thrusting his cock inside her.

Alexi screamed into his mouth at the feel of him inside her. God, it seemed like she'd been waiting forever to have him, and now that he was in her, she couldn't get enough.

They ravaged each other's mouths as they fucked. Alexi braced her hands on his shoulders, driving herself up and down on his cock, harder and faster. The spades bounced from her nipples and even the collar added to the extreme pleasure shooting through her body.

Darronn ripped his mouth from hers and captured her gaze. "Now, firecat!"

Alexi's climax blasted through her and she shrieked. Her cry echoed through the cavern, bouncing from crystal to crystal until the entire chamber sang. The harmony blended with the vibrancy of her orgasm and the purple and black crystals sparkled in tune with it all. Light, color, and sound blended into a symphony that set her world aflame.

CHAPTER TEN

S
TRAWBERRY TARTS RAINED FROM BLUE-GREEN
skies and scattered across the table where Alexi sat alone
in the middle of a forest. In front of her on the red tablecloth were a chipped plate and a cracked teacup resting on half
a saucer. Another place setting was arranged to her right, but
no one was sitting in the straight-backed chair.

Before Alexi could reach for one of the tarts, the sorceress appeared wearing nothing but an enormous stovepipe hat with a
wide brim. Even Kalina's collar and the spades that normally
dangled from her nipples were missing. In her hands was a tea-
pot with most of the spout broken off.

"All is not as it seems, Milady," Kalina said as she poured
tea into Alexi's cup. Fluid spilled over the teacup's brim, onto
the half saucer, then bled into the red tablecloth.

When the sorceress vanished, Alexi reached for one of the
tarts in the middle of the table, but before she could grasp the
tart it rose up in the air and settled on the plate to her right,
where someone was now sitting.

She raised her gaze to meet Alice's turquoise eyes.

Alexi gasped as she stared at her sister. Alice wore an almost sheer white dress with red hearts sprinkled over it. In her white-blond hair was the blue satin ribbon she'd been wearing the day of her disappearance.

Before she could jump up and throw herself at her twin, Alice held up her hand. In it was a black leather whip. "In Wonderland you must be careful," Alice said.

Chills rolled through Alexi as Alice laid the whip across the table and repeated the sorceress's warning, "All is not as it seems."

Alexi woke with a start. She blinked, her vision coming back into focus as the memory of where she was and what had happened returned to her.

That same awful ache settled in her gut because Alice wasn't really there with her. It had just been a freaking bizarre dream.

Yet it had seemed so real. And strangely enough, it made Alexi feel as if the connection she'd had with her twin from the time they were born until Alice vanished . . . it was as if that connection had been reestablished.

She had rarely remembered her dreams in the past, but the dream of her escape, and then this new dream of Alice were so clear and vivid in her mind.

Why?

Darronn stirred and her attention turned toward how good it felt to be in his embrace. His arm was draped around her waist, her back to his chest, his firm cock against her ass, and he had one leg hooked over her hip. Even in sleep he bound her to him, and she loved how it felt. They were lying on a fabulously soft black velvet cushion-bed that he had summoned with his magic and had arranged by the small waterfall.

His wonderful male musk surrounded her, making her feel both content and edgy all at once. He was an addiction to her system—yet she knew that it wasn't something that he'd forced on her. But he certainly could have long ago with that *tigri* pheromone. Good Lord, that had been an amazing experience. She couldn't help but respect the fact that in all the time she'd been here, he'd never used it to force her to want him.

Not that he'd had to force her, ever—even when he'd staked her to the ground all those weeks ago, she'd been unbelievably attracted to him. Darronn was every fantasy she'd ever had rolled into one amazingly muscled, powerful, gorgeous, and well-hung package.

His breath was warm on her nape, his breathing deep and even. She brought one hand to the collar still snug around her neck and ran a fingertip over the leather strap and the gold spades decorating it. At the same time she was very aware of the gold spades at her nipples that felt just as comfortable and familiar to her now as the tiger charm did at her navel.

Was something wrong with her, that she liked the collar and how the nipple rings felt? Knowing that they were signs of ownership should be demeaning, shouldn't it? That's what she'd thought when she'd watched Kalina walking around the château, and many of the other servants and villagers who wore collars and nipple piercings. Sure, they looked sexy, but she hadn't allowed herself to think of them beyond what convention dictated her thoughts should be.

Why does it feel so right to be wearing Darronn's signs of ownership now? Why do I enjoy the thought of belonging to him and only *him?*

Alexi was also amazed at how wonderful it felt to be able to truly count on someone to take care of her, someone who was her equal in every way. Choosing to submit to him felt delicious and special.

If only he would tell her that he loved her.

She knew how much he desired her, and she knew how much it pleased him that she had admitted her love.

But did he feel it in his heart and soul, too? He was so damn arrogant he probably expected it. But if he didn't love her, could she accept that?

No. Absolutely not. The answer was as clear as the feelings in Alexi's heart for her lover. If Darronn merely considered her a prize, or his due, she couldn't and wouldn't live with or accept it. She deserved to have her love returned a hundred percent, and she would settle for nothing less.

For a while Alexi watched the cavern's purple and black crystals glittering around her, and they reminded her a bit of the day the mirror had appeared in her bedroom. It seemed so long ago now, another lifetime. According to Kalina, the four weeks she'd spent in Tarok equated to a little over six Earth weeks . . . and in that short amount of time she'd lived with and had grown to love Darronn.

His words came back to her, from that first day in the meadow, *"For your own good, you must learn the desires and fears of your heart—and you must learn to trust and respect the one person with the skill and power to make you whole."*

Loving Darronn had allowed that and more. She did trust and respect him, but she would be whole only when he returned her love, and when she found Alice.

When Alexi's thoughts turned to her sister, thoughts of the dream came back to her and that familiar ache returned deep in the pit of her stomach and in her heart. Alice deserved someone special, too—especially after the assholes who had hurt her so badly.

Damn it. What happened to Alice? Where is she now?

Alexi squeezed her eyes shut and bit the inside of her cheek. For crissake, she wasn't the crying type, and she wasn't about to start now. For the past year she'd let her anger drive her as she searched for Alice, and not once had she stopped long enough to let the pain take over and control her.

But right now Alexi felt like she was anything but in control. And in reality, she never had been. She'd tried and tried, and nothing she'd done had worked.

What would it be like to turn everything over to someone else, or to at least turn some things over? To stop trying to fight the world on her own . . . and maybe allow someone to help her fight her battles . . . or fight them for her.

The moment Darronn woke, he sensed that his mate

was in turmoil. She had admitted her love for him and had chosen to wear his signs of ownership . . . what could cause her to feel such distress that it vibrated through his very being?

"Firecat," he murmured as he rolled her onto her back and positioned himself between her thighs in a smooth motion. "What troubles your heart?"

Her normally strong and confident expression had vanished, and in its place was the vulnerable look of a woman who needed him. Her aqua eyes were bright as though unshed tears glistened there. "My sister. It's been so long. I need to find her."

For a moment Darronn considered telling her that her sister was safe and well, but he decided now was not the time. She would want to leave at once and he first needed to meet with his brothers. Ty and Karn would be arriving from their respective kingdoms in the next day or so. Once they had determined their next course of action against Mikaela, Darronn would tell Alexi. It would be soon enough and he would then be ready to make the journey to Hearts with her.

"Trust me, firecat." He slid his cock into her channel still slick with their lovemaking, ensuring she would not dwell upon such thoughts for now. "You shall see your sister again."

Alexi gasped as Darronn filled her, and he smiled at the power he had over her. Her scent of starflower and midnight only made him hungrier for her, and he knew he would never get enough of her.

She clamped her thighs tight around his hips as he

took both her wrists with one hand and pinned them above her head, fastening her gold bracelets together with his magic. Seeing his collar at her throat and his rings at her nipples gave him a feeling of intense pride. He was certainly the most blessed of men to have such a fine woman as his possession.

Well, not exactly his possession. His . . . mate.

Her eyes were wide and filled with emotion and trust that he had not witnessed in their depths before. "I love you, Darronn," she whispered as he slowly drove in and out of her. "I never thought I would care for anyone the way I love you."

"I will always take care of you." He gave her a slow and sensual smile as he focused his gaze on hers and increased the strength of his thrusts. "And you will always be able to trust me with your love."

"Darronn!" Alexi cried out as he pounded his cock into her. "Just know this," she said, her voice quavering with passion, "if you break my heart, I'll kick your ass."

The fire and strength in his woman pleased him to the depths of his soul and filled him with a power like none he had ever felt in his many years. "Come for me, Alexi," he demanded, never taking his gaze from her beautiful face and never slowing his thrusts.

Her eyes widened as though in surprise that his voice could command her orgasm. She trembled and arched up her breasts as she cried out. A flush stole across her skin and her body glistened with sweat as her climax shook her.

Darronn's own orgasm rushed over him like a raging

wildfire. Furious and fast it came, and he roared as his fluid spilled into his woman.

When at last he was spent, he rolled onto his side and cradled Alexi close to him, his cock still snug inside her quim. She sighed and snuggled into him, and his feelings of power and possessiveness grew.

The cards had indeed given him the woman who was his perfect mate.

Just days after Alexi had proclaimed her love for him, Darronn strode from his chambers and left his mate to her own devices. His boots echoed down the granite hall as he headed toward the sorceress Kalina's quarters to meet with his brothers Ty and Karn, who had recently arrived with news from Jarronn.

Alexi's sweet scent was still on Darronn's skin and he pictured her as he had left her, sprawled upon their bed, naked and well sated. He no longer felt concern that she would attempt to escape again. Nay, after their time in the cavern she seemed more content to stay in Spades, if not truly happy, and that pleased him greatly.

While he strode to the other end of the château, he smiled at the memory of his time with Alexi. Soon he would tell Alexi of her sister's fate and take his future queen to Hearts to visit High Queen Alice. He wished to ensure that Alexi was tightly bonded to him before they made the journey, and to do that he needed her full attention, her complete devotion.

All was going exactly as he had planned.

He raked his hand through his wild mane of hair as he neared the sorceress's chambers. The past few days had been full of unparalleled pleasure and enjoyment for Darronn and Alexi. They had spent much time discussing their lives and what they had done before he brought her to Tarok, and their bond had grown even tighter.

Darronn had recognized long ago that she would never be content to serve only as his mate. But as his queen she would rule at his side and he was certain she would enjoy the role. His people already loved her spirit, and when they witnessed her wearing his signs of possession, they had felt as he did, that Alexi was now one of them and truly belonged in their world.

The one thing that concerned him was that she seemed to have no desire for children. Alexi had been curious why there were none in his kingdom, and he had explained about the Queen of Malachad and what she had done to his people. How she had used her legions of *bakirs* and mindspells to invade the dreams of the women of Tarok and caused them to become infertile.

Darronn would not force Alexi to bear his children, even if it meant his people would one day be gone with no one to carry on into the future.

When he strode into the sorceress's dim chambers, smells of almond, vanilla, and sandalwood washed over him. Kalina's beautiful face was illuminated by the glowing *a'bin*, the table she used to foretell the destiny of all four kingdoms throughout the lands of Tarok. Upon it were magical cards she was studying, each bearing pictures that swirled with thousands of images whose mysteries only Kalina could unravel.

Karn had one shoulder hitched against the wall as he studied the lovely sorceress while she worked. The look in his dark eyes was one that Darronn hadn't seen since the wars with Mikaela the previous summer, and that troubled him greatly.

Ty, the youngest of the four kings, was missing the roguish expression that he usually had, his golden head tilted to one side and his arms folded across his broad chest.

Karn flicked his gaze from Kalina to Darronn, a slight raise of his eyebrows the only sign of greeting before he looked back to the sorceress. Ty merely gave Darronn an abrupt nod. Darronn's gut clenched, and he had no doubt the sorceress's news would not be good.

When he stood before the table, he clasped his hands behind his back and waited for Kalina's trance to end. Her dark brows puckered in concentration, her gaze darting from one card to the next. Beneath the scant leather clothing she wore, her chest rose and fell, the dark circles around her nipples peeking above and below the thin strip of leather that bound her breasts. It occurred to him that at one time the sight would have aroused him, yet now it caused him only to think of Alexi and how much he desired to return to her.

At great length Kalina raised her fire-ice eyes and met his gaze. "The cards hold tight to their secrets, Master. However, it is clear Mikaela will strike soon. I am not positive where the true peril lies, but I fear that Queen Alice and her cubs are in great danger."

Karn and Ty both growled aloud at the news. Rage flamed through Darronn and he barely reined in his fury. "When?" he asked through clenched teeth.

"Soon." Kalina glanced to the cards and back to Darronn, then to Karn and Ty. "You must return to Hearts if the High Queen and her cubs are to survive. Of this I am certain."

After taking a quick bath, Alexi slipped on one of her favorite leather outfits and clasped on the leather and gold collar. When she glanced at her reflection in the mirror, she liked how it looked on her—kind of sexy. She still had a few scratches on her body from climbing down the ravenwood trellis, but they didn't look too bad and they no longer itched.

A smile touched her lips as she thought about the past few days and how much closer she and Darronn had grown. She couldn't believe how happy she was with him. She'd finally met the man who was her equal in every way. Someone she loved, trusted, and respected. The only thing that marred her happiness was that he had yet to tell her he loved her.

Her smile turned into a small frown. Well, she certainly wasn't going to beg for his love. And she needed to have a serious talk with him about either letting her go in search of her sister, or maybe helping her find Alice.

The thought of Darronn stalking the streets of San Francisco caused her to grin. Talk about a fish out of water. Or rather a tiger out of his realm.

When she was dressed and her hair combed, Alexi set out in search of Kalina. She'd heard a lot about the sorceress's abilities, so maybe she could help. With Darronn always around, Alexi never had the chance to be alone with Kalina, but she had the feeling that today would be different.

Alexi wasn't used to sitting around and waiting for things to happen. She *made* things happen. These weeks in Spades had been strange and exciting, but it was time she got back on track. Hopefully with Darronn's support, she would do so once she had a concrete plan of action.

As she approached Kalina's quarters, Alexi caught the sound of male voices along with Kalina's and she frowned. Was the sorceress busy screwing a couple of guys? Damn. She'd have to come back.

But when Alexi caught Darronn's voice, her stomach clenched. No, she could trust him, she knew he wouldn't . . . although they had never discussed an exclusive relationship. She'd just assumed.

She didn't bother to peek around the corner to see what was going on. She walked right into the room and stopped at the doorway. Darronn and two other gorgeous men were involved in a heated discussion, and she recognized them both from their portraits. Of course, Darronn, with his wood-brown hair, with his golden earring and spade tattoo, was by far the best looking as far as she was concerned.

Karn, the King of Diamonds, was bare from the waist up. He was the dark-haired brother with a diamond tattoo on the back of his right shoulder, and he wore an intense expression, as if really concerned about something.

Ty, the King of Clubs and the youngest brother, was the opposite in coloring with blond hair, and of course he had a club tattoo. The devilish smile he'd had in the portrait was missing, though, and it was replaced with a look of frustration.

The sorceress's golden eyes met Alexi's, but the men didn't notice her.

Alexi's first reaction was relief—all the men had their clothes on, and so did Kalina.

However, when she caught what the men were saying, her skin flushed with heat, and then went cold, cold, cold.

"We must leave for Hearts at once," the black-haired king was saying. "Queen Alice must be protected at all costs."

"Her cubs as well," the blond king added with an emphatic nod.

Darronn's scowl was fierce. "We will allow no harm to come to our brother's mate and my future queen's sibling."

In that one crystallized moment, suspended in space and time as if by a single thread, everything became clear to Alexi.

Her ears buzzed and her vision narrowed to only the three men, and then to her supposed lover.

Darronn's assurances that she would one day see Alice again . . .

His lack of concern about finding her sister . . .

The son of a bitch had known all along where Alice was because she'd been kidnapped into this freaked-out world, too.

He had known, and he had let her suffer all this time, battling her loyalties and heart—for what? To prove to himself she loved him more than she loved her sister? To show his total dominance and control over her?

"You bastard," Alexi said with such venom that all conversation in the room came to an abrupt halt and the men turned to look at her. She ignored everyone else as she marched up to Darronn with her fists clenched. "You're the man who said he'd teach me a thing or two about trust and respect. You lying fucker!"

He frowned. "Firecat—"

"Don't you call me that *ever* again." Fury poured through her in such waves that she trembled from head to toe.

All the days and nights of pain and uncertainty. Of missing her sister so badly her gut felt torn in two.

He had known where she was from day one. From before day one!

Growling like a tiger herself, Alexi reached up and grasped the fastening of her collar and yanked it off. "I accepted this from the man I thought was honest and trustworthy." She flung it at his feet and it landed on his boots. "Obviously you're not the man I thought you were. You love no one but yourself, and you do only what will further *your* needs and *your* desires. You think everything that comes to you is your due, don't you? Well, let's just make this plenty clear for you, asshole. I don't want anything to do with you."

With all her might she slammed her fist against his jaw, causing his head to turn only slightly from the force of her punch. The pain in her hand was intense and immediate, but she ignored it. Darronn slowly looked back at her, his expression a mask of no emotion.

"How dare you strike a Tarok King, wench?" The blond man stepped forward and grabbed her forearm, his eyes flaring with anger.

"Fuck off." At the same moment she jerked her arm away from the blond, she swung her knee up and into his balls.

The man blanched and was obviously so taken by surprise that she easily freed her wrist.

Alexi turned her glare back on Darronn. "I'm leaving now for this place called Hearts to get my sister and to get the hell out of here." She backed away as she spoke, and he only stared at her now, making no move to speak or to follow her. "Even if I have to fuck someone to take me there, I'll find a way. And this time you'd better not follow me. You'd better not come near me!"

With that she turned her back on the bastard, and holding her chin high she left to go find Alice, once and for all.

CHAPTER ELEVEN

"WOULD YOU LIKE ME TO GO AFTER THE MAID and bring her back?" Karn said in a low tone as Ty, clearly incapable of speech, braced one hand against the wall and clenched his teeth.

"Do you wish to have your bollocks crushed?" Darronn grumbled as his gaze followed Alexi from the room. "My firecat would most certainly see to it."

The corner of Karn's mouth quirked as he glanced at Ty, who looked like he had yet to breathe since Alexi kneed him in his groin.

With a slow shake of his head, Darronn said, "As my mate Alexi owes no one but me her submission. And she does not even owe me that because I failed to earn it."

He turned his eyes on Kalina, who stood quietly beside the *a'bin* awaiting his instructions. "Make whatever preparations are necessary and then take Kira to escort Alexi to Hearts with the *jul*. I will follow to ensure the safety of all, but out of sight so that my mate is unaware."

"Yes, Master." Kalina bowed and slipped from the room.

"You will just let the wench strike two of Tarok's Kings?" Ty asked after the sorceress had gone, his voice a shade higher than normal.

Darronn turned the force of his frustration on his brother. "I did not ask for your interference, and you received your due." Darronn ran his hand over his stubbled jaw that still throbbed from Alexi's blow. "As I received mine. The maid spoke only the truth, and she was right to be angry."

His gut clenched with pain unlike any he had experienced in his many years. When Darronn spoke again, his voice was harsh with the realization that he may have lost the only woman he had ever loved, or would again. "My only hope is that it is not too late to win back her heart . . . and to give her mine."

Alexi was so furious as she marched back to their—*Darronn's*—chambers that she could barely see straight. Her knuckles throbbed from hitting his jaw, and as hard as she'd rammed her knee into blondy's balls, it was a wonder her knee didn't ache, too.

Even as angry as she was, she was still stunned and hurt that he'd allowed her to continue going through hell. All this time he'd known where Alice was.

The bastard! Well, she was going to grab what she needed and get the hell out of there.

Only when she got to the room she realized she had

no decent clothing to travel in. "Goddamn him," she muttered as she went to the trunk where he kept his clothing stashed. He was so huge she'd never fit into his pants, but his tunic would certainly cover more than these stupid-ass leather outfits he'd given her. His intoxicating scent flowed over her as she grabbed one of his black leather shirts from the trunk, and she had to bite her lip to keep it from trembling.

What the hell is the matter with me? She never cried, and she certainly wouldn't waste one single tear over the likes of his Royal Assness, Darronn of Spades.

After she stripped out of her clothing, Alexi plucked off the spade nipple rings and threw them onto the bed with such vehemence they bounced across the surface and landed onto the granite floor with soft tinkling sounds. She was about to yank on Darronn's shirt when Kalina entered the room carrying a bundle of black leather and a pair of boots. The sorceress was wearing more clothes than Alexi had seen any woman wear in Spades since she'd arrived. Kalina had dressed entirely in black with tight leather pants, a leather shirt and jacket, and leather boots that laced up to her knees. A golden sword hilt thrust up from a leather scabbard at her side, and the gold spades glittered from the collar still at her throat.

"What do you want?" Alexi growled at the sorceress.

Kalina tossed the bundle on the bed and her amber eyes met Alexi's. "I have brought suitable clothing for travel. Kira is gathering enough food for the journey and will meet us at the stables."

"What do you mean *us?*" Alexi didn't bother to thank the sorceress as she snatched the pair of pants from the bed and tugged them on. "You knew all along that Alice is in Hearts, didn't you?"

"Yes," Kalina said quietly. "I am very fond of the High Queen, and it has greatly pained my soul to be unable to share with you news of your sister."

So many thoughts rambled through Alexi's mind from all that she'd heard since walking in on Darronn and his little meeting. *High Queen . . . Queen Alice's cubs . . .*

But for now Alexi chose to ignore the many questions and to focus instead on getting to her sister.

"Then why didn't you tell me about her?" Alexi yanked on the tunic and tucked it into the pants. The clothing was snug, a perfect fit. "You're not a slave. You have a mind of your own."

"I serve my king," Kalina replied, calm confidence in her voice as Alexi pulled on the boots. "I may not always agree with his decisions, but I trust him to do what he believes is right. King Darronn is a good man, Alexi. But he is a man, and men do make mistakes."

"He sure as hell did with me." Alexi finished lacing up her boots and scooped up a leather binding that Darronn had used to tie her up with only that morning. With a few efficient movements, she plaited her hair into a single thick braid and used the strip of leather to tie the end.

She paused to glance at her reflection in the mirror. She looked like she could spit bricks and take out an army of commandos on her own. With a little weaponry she could even pass for Lara Croft from *Tomb Raider*.

Alexi turned back to the sorceress. "The bastard told you to take me to Hearts, didn't he?"

Kalina nodded. "It is not more than two days' journey, but it can be dangerous."

Alexi grabbed the jacket on the bed and strode toward the door. "He just didn't like the idea of me screwing another man to get there."

The sorceress gave a delicate little snort. Alexi glanced at her and caught the hint of a smile. "Indeed, Milady," Kalina said. "Indeed."

It had been nearly a full day since they had left the château, but Alexi had set a pace that would honor the finest of warriors, Darronn thought as he followed his woman. In their tiger forms, he and his brothers blended with the forest, silently weaving in and out of bushes and trees, ensuring Alexi never saw them. Ty guarded Kira, Karn trailed Kalina, and of course, Darronn never let Alexi out of his sight.

Alexi, Kalina, and Kira all rode the finest *jul* steeds with black saddles tooled with the Kingdom of Spades crest. The graceful beasts had the stamina of a hundred men and could go for days without food or water. Tok carried Alexi, his fine silver coat glittering in the dappled late afternoon sunshine. Kalina rode a golden *jul,* and a bronze-coated steed bore Kira. They were not chameleons, but the *jul* had the unique ability to blend with the forest, to become a part of the sunshine or starlight as they traveled.

In his tiger form, Darronn was able to communicate with Kalina in thought-words, instructing her to encourage Alexi to make camp before they left the cover of the forest. Tomorrow would be a day's journey across the plains before they arrived in Hearts.

While they traveled, Darronn worked over and over in his mind the mistake he had made with Alexi. He had known she had difficulty with trust, yet he had broken her faith in him. Because of his arrogance he had thought he knew what was best for her. And mayhap it was because he feared this very thing might happen . . . that he would lose her.

No matter. He had done the unforgivable. He had denied her vital information, and in doing so he had violated the most basic tenet of trust in any relationship where power was so totally shared and transferred— her ability to give a full and informed consent to Darronn's choices for them as a couple.

And when she found out what he had held back, the second basic tenet had been destroyed—trust.

A growl rose up within his throat and he barely contained it. Whatever it took, he would win her back.

When it was dusk, Alexi and her companions neared the edge of the forest. The women had scarcely spoken since leaving Spades and the only noises were the soft thuds of the *jul*'s hooves upon the forest loam and the calls of night birds.

"It would be best to make camp here for the night," Kalina suggested in her calm yet concerned tone. "It is not safe to cross the plains in the dark."

Alexi only nodded her agreement—she hadn't been in the mood to talk all day. Her mind had been too busy going over everything, and her heart alternated from heaviness over Darronn's betrayal to excitement that she would see Alice soon.

As she dismounted from Tok, Alexi's muscles complained and she ached from her neck to her ass to her legs. The leather saddle had been comfortable while she traveled, but now she was walking bowlegged. Who knew that riding a horse—er, *jul*—could be so exhausting? It reminded her of when she'd learned how to ride her Harley and had gone on her first all-day excursion.

Her knuckles still throbbed from slugging Darronn, but that only caused her to give a satisfied smile. *The bastard.*

"If you do not mind, Milady," Kalina said as she removed the saddle from her *jul*, "you could spread out our bedding there, beside those boulders, while Kira gathers firewood. I will unsaddle the *jul* and brush them down."

"Sure," Alexi said, her muscles griping as she snatched up a bedroll and took it over to the boulders. It felt good to keep busy, to know that she was working toward a goal.

Yet as she helped Kira and Kalina set up their camp for the night, Alexi couldn't help but feel an ache in her heart. She had given her love to Darronn, and he had betrayed that love and her trust in him. How could he have done that to her after knowing what she'd gone through, and how she'd thought she'd never trust anyone again?

Even though she was furious at Darronn, Alexi felt an excitement and happiness that she hadn't felt for over a year. *Alice is alive!* She couldn't wait to find her sister and take her home to San Francisco. Although that thing about her being High Queen and having cubs seemed a little troubling—and might even throw a wrench in the works.

After their bedrolls were spread out around a small campfire, and after Alexi had found a nearby bush to relieve herself, the women ate the hot dinner Kira had cooked.

When they finished eating, Alexi sat on a flat rock a little bit away from the other two, who quietly chatted and laughed. For a moment she stared at her gold bracelets that all but glowed in the firelight, and she couldn't help but think about all the times Darronn had fastened them together with his magic.

No! Don't think about that—that ass.

Alexi forced herself to turn her thoughts back to her sister, which wasn't really hard at all. She had so many questions.

"Alice has children?" Alexi finally asked, interrupting the women.

Both grew quiet, and then Kalina smiled—and it was so radiant that it nearly stole Alexi's breath. "Your niece and nephew are beautiful children, Milady. And they are such a joy to your sister and her king."

Alexi had to absorb what Kalina was saying for a moment. "Alice is married to the King of Hearts, who's also the High King?"

"They are bonded, yes." Kalina stood and walked to where Alexi sat upon the boulder and settled beside her. "The Queen is very much in love with Jarronn, and he in turn loves her with all his heart."

"Wow." Alexi shook her head, trying to come to grips with this strange new reality. "I don't even know what to think right now."

Cupping Alexi's cheek with one hand, Kalina forced Alexi to look into her fiery amber eyes. "Queen Alice has missed you as much as you have missed her, I am certain. But she is also happier than she has ever been in her young life. I hope that pleases you."

Alexi leaned into Kalina's comforting touch, needing the human contact for a moment. She missed her sister, missed her cousin and aunt, and damn it, she missed Darronn, too.

"Alice's happiness is really all that matters," Alexi whispered, and struggled to keep her voice from cracking. "That's all I've ever wanted."

"I know." Kalina smiled. "You will be pleased with her cubs, as well. They are most beautiful and quite lively."

Withdrawing from the sorceress's touch, Alexi blew a puff of air that caused her hair to fly out of her eyes. "I'm an aunt . . . to twin cubs?"

Kalina laughed and settled her hands in her lap. "Weretiger cubs, yes."

"So do they look just like little tigers or something?"

"When they were born, they were tiny helpless humans, just like you were as an infant." Kalina tossed her long black hair over her shoulder with a flick of her hand. "But when they reached nine Tarok months of age, they began to shift into tigers. A handful they are for their mother and father, I'm sure you can imagine."

Alexi tried to picture chasing after two little tigers herself. "Uh, no." She rolled her eyes. "That image just does not compute."

Kalina laughed again, and Alexi stifled a yawn and murmured, "Damn, but I'm tired."

Only rather than going to bed, Kira and Kalina both began to help each other strip out of their clothing— and they were *fondling* each other as they undressed. Alexi's jaw dropped at the sensual play between the two women. She'd known, and had witnessed from her balcony, that in Spades it didn't matter if you were woman or man, everyone enjoyed one another's pleasures. She also knew that plenty of ménages happened as part of the norm.

That had never been Alexi's style—maybe she was just too possessive, but she was a one-man kinda gal and she didn't like the idea of sharing. Just the thought of Darronn being with another woman—

Alexi squeezed her eyes shut, forcing away the thought and the ache in her heart. It didn't matter anymore what Darronn did or with who, because she was through with him.

Kalina moaned and Alexi opened one eye to see Kira suckling Kalina's nipple. The sorceress's head was tipped back and she grasped Kira's hips tightly to hers. The two women were completely naked now, except for their leather collars and nipple charms, their bodies illuminated by the light of the fire.

Alexi swallowed and opened her other eye. Damn, but she never thought it would be arousing to watch two beautiful naked women together, but she had to admit it was.

"Please join us, Milady," Kalina said, shattering Alexi's trance.

"Um, thanks, but no." Alexi glanced around the dark forest as if looking for an escape route, before returning her gaze to the sorceress. "Someone needs to watch camp. Keep an eye on things."

A mischievous smile lifted the corner of Kalina's sensual mouth as she brought her hands to Kira's full breasts and teased the spades at her nipples. "Do not worry. Camp is being watched, and we are safe."

It took a moment for Kalina's meaning to sink in and then Alexi went still. "Darronn and those other kings, they followed us, didn't they?"

"Please do not be upset," Kalina said. "He only wishes to protect you from harm."

Alexi buried her face in her hands. For one, she couldn't take the sight of the women enjoying a little sex when she was getting none, and for another, she couldn't believe she'd been stupid enough to think that Darronn would just let her go.

That thought was frustrating, comforting, and even exhilarating all at once. He shouldn't have followed her! Yet maybe he realized how badly he'd screwed up, and he wasn't sure how to fix it. But he respected her enough to not shove it down her throat.

Or maybe he realized she wasn't what he wanted and he was going to let her go, but was just making sure she was safe.

Alexi pushed that last thought right out of her head. She was too self-confident to allow that kind of thinking to tear at her. She'd made up her mind about Darronn before—he either returned her love, or he didn't and she'd move on. The trust thing . . . that had blindsided her, though. She wasn't sure she could get past that.

"Would you mind, Milady"—Kalina's skin was flushed and her voice breathless as she gestured toward the forest—"if Kira and I join Ty and Karn?"

"Sure, go have a good fuck." Alexi waved them off. "Have an orgasm for me while you're at it."

When the women vanished into the trees, Alexi slid off her boulder and onto the bedroll at her feet. She wrapped her arms around her bent legs and rested her chin on her knees.

Alexi could sense Darronn watching her, hungering for her. Her body ached for him, but she wasn't about to give in to lust. Not after what he'd done, and not at the expense of her heart.

CHAPTER TWELVE

ARRONN WASN'T SURE WHETHER TO REWARD Kalina for informing Alexi that he had followed them, or to throttle her. However, the mischievous look on the sorceress's face told him she was looking forward to sensual punishment at Karn's hands, and the King of Diamonds would no doubt enjoy seeing to Kalina's punishment and pleasure.

Fair enough. Leave her to Karn, for I have no desire to touch any but my own mate.

While the sounds of sex from his brothers and the women nearly drove him mad with lust for his woman, Darronn watched Alexi. Staying well hidden, he remained a tiger and studied her from the dark forest. He had expected anger from her when she learned he had followed her, but again she surprised him.

She seems . . . relieved.

And perhaps intrigued?

A feeling of hope rose within his soul. Mayhap she

would forgive him, and would take him back. He could not force her, but his heart would not allow him to let her go.

For a long while Alexi stared into the fire's dancing flames, her arms wrapped around her bent legs and her chin resting on her knees, and Darronn could not take his gaze from her. Patience had never been his virtue, nor had tolerating uncertainty. After Mikaela's betrayal he hadn't thought himself capable of giving any woman leeway, much less access to his heart.

This woman, though . . .

He felt a purr build in his veins.

This woman was worth any risk, and any wait.

The crackle and hiss of burning wood joined the night song of crickets, the roar of the Tarok River, and wind stirring the trees. Over the ridge came a mountain wolf's call, and Darronn recognized Kir's howl. Annoyance clouded his thoughts. Why was the werewolf lord so far out of his own territory?

Alexi noticed the sound, as well. She shivered and seemed mildly distressed. Darronn sensed more than saw her glance in his direction.

Yes, my love. No matter the state of affairs between us, I will protect you with my very life.

While he watched Alexi, Darronn hoped she would choose to call to him, to give some indication that she wanted him as badly as he needed her. She was so small and beautiful, yet she had the will of the strongest of beings and a temper to match.

But instead of asking him to join her, Alexi gave a

long sigh, then crawled between the folds of her bedroll, covering herself from head to toe.

Darronn settled his head on his paws, never taking his gaze from her form. He wished to go to her, to hold her tight in his embrace. But he would wait until she was ready. He would wait as long as needed to win her back.

When Alexi woke, gray dawn had crept through the forest. Blue-green mist clung to trees, a chill had stolen through her covering, and her nose was cold. A light scampering came from overhead and she wondered if perhaps it was a squirrel, or some unusual Tarok forest creature. One of the *jul* whickered nearby and another answered him with a soft whinny.

The fire was burning still and Alexi wondered if the men had continued to add fuel to it during the night. Had Darronn perhaps tended the blaze, and had he even watched her as she slept?

It had taken her a while to fall asleep, knowing that he was so close. How could she want him still? Yet her body ached for his touch and for those wicked green eyes that devoured her every time he looked at her. She missed his muscled form against her back, his cock pressed to her hip and rarin' to go. A part of her even wished that he had stolen into camp during the night and curled around her in his tiger form.

Another part of her wanted to kick him in the nuts.

Damn him! Why did he have to screw everything up?

Both Kira and Kalina stirred as Alexi's thoughts

centered on Darronn, and soon the two women were up and about, fully clothed and ready for the day. Apparently after their sexathon they had dressed in their leather outfits again. Alexi crawled out of her bedroll and helped them prepare breakfast and pack their belongings. She expected the men to appear for food, but then she realized they'd probably hunted for fresh meat during the night.

When she crept behind a bush to pee, she grumbled loud enough that she knew Darronn could hear, "You'd better not be watching me, you overgrown moth-eaten fur coat."

She thought she heard a soft growl, but she didn't look in the direction it came from and hurried about her business. When she went back to camp, she refused to look anywhere but straight ahead. She didn't want to see Darronn in the trees or underbrush as man or tiger, and she didn't want to meet that striking green gaze of his.

The women set out when it was still early enough that the sun was just peering over the horizon. Both Kalina and Kira seemed quieter, focused, and quite relaxed.

Nothing like having a wild night of orgasms.

Alexi, though, was on edge. Her nipples and pussy ached for Darronn, and it was pissing her off. Last night she should have masturbated beneath her blanket to take the edge off her need. Hell, she should have done it in front of him, just to let him see what he was missing and what he wasn't going to get.

The women guided their horselike beasts through

the remainder of the Tarok Forest, nearing the river, its ever-present roar growing louder. Even though she was saddle sore from yesterday, and her knuckles still throbbed, she felt rested and exhilarated, ready to see her sister. That happiness kept at bay the pain of Darronn's betrayal of her trust in him.

Alice is only a day away, her heart sang. God, what an incredible relief to know that after over a year since her sister's disappearance, she was alive!

Sharp wind blew at their backs as they reached the end of the forest and stopped in a clearing just shy of the plains. Yellowed grass rippled like golden waves for miles ahead of them. A melody like the sound of a violin swelled across the plains and joined the river's harmony.

Kira and Kalina's mounts paused to either side of Alexi. "The Singing Plains," Kalina said with a smile to Alexi. "On a windy day such as this, its music is most beautiful."

The wind shifted, blowing full in Alexi's face, and she caught a scent she couldn't identify. Tok whinnied loud and shrill, like a warning. Metal glinted in the morning sunlight as the women of Spades withdrew their swords in lightning-fast motions.

"Damnation," Kalina said, her voice filled with concern. "Do not let her into your mind, Milady."

"What—" Alexi started, then sucked in her breath as she saw them.

Dozens of white tigers rose up from where they'd been hiding in the tall grass. In seconds the beasts had surrounded the women and the *jul,* cutting them off from Darronn and his brothers. The ring of tigers was at least three deep, and by their fierce expressions and rumbling growls, Alexi knew that she and her companions were in deep shit.

Adrenaline pumped through Alexi and she gripped Tok's reins so tight that her knuckles ached. The furious pounding of her heart multiplied when a pure white tiger with no stripes pushed its way through the ring of tigers and came into the clearing and stopped before Tok. Before Alexi could process what was happening, the tiger shifted, rising up on its hind legs as its features morphed from white fur to skin, from tiger to woman.

The slender woman held a long black whip in one hand, her other hand propped on her leather-clad hip. Her wheat-blond hair stirred in the wind and her full breasts almost spilled from the V neckline of her tight black leather pantsuit. The neckline was so wide the woman's dark areolas partially showed, and the V dropped to a tattoo of a large cat's paw print around her belly button.

Alexi didn't have time for this crap. She needed to get to her sister. "Who the hell are you?" she asked, her glare meeting the woman's ice-blue gaze.

"I am Mikaela, Queen of Malachad." Irritation glittered in the woman's eyes, but it was replaced by a look of smug confidence. "I have come to assist you in returning to your home. I called to you in your dreams . . . where I showed you the looking glass in the meadow."

Alexi's jaw dropped. *What the hell? How does this Mi-*

kaela know about my dreams? Her gaze rested on the whip in the woman's hands and the dream of Alice and her warning caused a chill to skitter down Alexi's spine.

A tickling sensation crawled at the back of her head, like a spider walking up her brain stem. Kalina's warning flashed through Alexi's memory: *Do not let her into your mind, Milady.*

"I don't give a damn who you are." Alexi's temper flared and she leaned forward in her saddle. "You're in my way."

Mikaela looked at her for a long moment. "You are far stronger than your sister." In a movement that seemed unconscious, the woman began lightly slapping the handle of the whip against her palm as she studied Alexi. "Alice is fat and weak."

Fury burned through Alexi. "Listen, bitch," she shot back with a scowl. "Don't you *ever* talk about my sister that way."

The woman snapped her whip so fast that Alexi didn't even see it coming. The leather strap wrapped around her waist and Mikaela yanked so hard that Alexi flew from her saddle. Pain shot through her as she landed flat on her back in front of the line of ferocious and hungry-looking tigers.

Alexi scrambled to her feet, so furious she could barely see. In the same motion with which she'd pulled Alexi from the saddle, Mikaela had unraveled her whip and now stood poised to strike again.

"I would kill you now if I did not have better use for you than as a carcass," Mikaela said as she came so close that Alexi could see silver flecks in the woman's blue eyes. "How it will torture my brother to know that his woman is being fucked by my *bakirs*."

Mikaela raised her whip, but this time Alexi was faster. She slammed her fist as hard as she could into the woman's eye and drove her other fist into Mikaela's belly.

The bitch screamed and toppled backward. Yet somehow she managed to snake her whip around Alexi's throat.

Fire burned Alexi's neck and her throat closed off as she was forced down onto her hands and knees. She clawed at the whip, her vision dimming as the leather strangled her.

Everything around her blurred as she fought for breath. Kalina's scream and the sudden thunder of countless roars seemed miles away.

And then she saw tigers closing in on her.

When Mikaela's weretigers rose up from the grass, Darronn's gut clenched and rage seared his soul. His first instinct was to charge forward to protect his woman. But common sense and his warrior's instincts prevailed. He could not even engage in thought-words with his brothers for fear that any one of the weretigers or Mikaela would hear him.

From where he was hiding in the forest, Darronn neared the ring of tigers, hoping that he could pass for one of Mikaela's *bakirs*. If any of them recognized his scent, they would attack at once, and Alexi would be in even greater danger.

His heart pounded and fear for his mate grew as he slipped into the ring of tigers and heard Alexi's words of fury to Mikaela. His anger magnified as his mate's cry tore across the plains and as he saw her fall from Tok's back and heard the thump of her body as she landed on the ground.

To the dark hells, Darronn thought as he bunched his muscles, prepared to spring forward and rush to his mate.

But one of Mikaela's tiger's whirled on Darronn, striking out with sharp claws and teeth and a roar that alerted the other weretigers.

Darronn ignored the pain as claws raked his cheek and shredded flesh and fur. He drove his muzzle into the tiger's neck in a furious motion and ripped open its throat. Another tiger attacked Darronn, and around him rose the sounds of roars and fighting. He and his brothers were fierce warriors, but they were far outnumbered. Sheer rage and the desire to save his mate propelled him forward despite the odds.

A wolf's howl tore through the melee and then the answering howl of countless werewolves. *Lord Kir!* The werewolf lord and his pack had come to join in the battle against Mikaela.

Claws shredded Darronn's flesh but he destroyed one weretiger after another until he reached the innermost ring. Even as he continued to fight, he saw Mikaela with her whip wrapped around Alexi's neck. His mate was on her belly, her features a ghastly shade of purple, her aqua eyes large and glossy as her gaze met his.

From their saddles Kalina and Kira dispatched tiger after tiger with their swords. The tigers had blocked the Spades women and Tok from reaching Mikaela and helping Alexi. Tok and the other two *jul* steeds lashed out with hooves, but even their fine coats were bloody.

Three weretigers pounced on Darronn at once and with a mighty roar he fought them off. His fury was so great at seeing his mate nearly strangled that his strength was that of a dozen weretigers. In quick, efficient movements he eliminated his opponents and charged toward Mikaela, the sister he had once loved.

The betraying bitch.

Mikaela shifted into a white tigress and bolted into the maelstrom of fighting weretigers and werewolves. Darronn started to charge after her but went to his mate instead. He shifted into his man form, withdrawing his sword and fighting off tigers even as he reached Alexi. Ty and Karn arrived in the inner circle and battled any beast that came near as Darronn slit the leather binding his woman's throat.

In a rush he rose back up, prepared to fight more of Mikaela's minions when he saw that the fighting had all but ended. Werewolves chased the remaining weretigers into the forest and the tall grasses of the plains. Bodies of both tigers and wolves were strewn everywhere and blood soaked the clearing's pale ground.

Darronn knelt beside his mate. Alexi's body was limp, her face now pale instead of the horrid color it had been.

With more fear than he remembered feeling in his long life, Darronn checked the pulse at her throat. Relief unlike anything he had ever known filled him in a heated rush.

"Wake, my love." Darronn gathered Alexi into his arms and held her tight to his chest. He kissed her forehead. "You *must* come back to me."

Alexi moaned and her eyelids fluttered. "Darronn?" she whispered.

Intense joy filled him at the sound of his name upon her tongue. "Whatever you desire in this or any world, it is yours." He brushed his lips over hers and murmured, "I love you, Alexi. My heart and soul belong to you."

He pulled away to meet her gaze. "Bastard," she said, her voice hoarse from the near strangulation. The corner of her mouth quirked and she added, "You'd better remember that promise. I intend to make you keep it."

CHAPTER THIRTEEN

E VEN THOUGH ALEXI HAD BEEN ANXIOUS TO
hurry to Hearts to see her sister, she realized
it was necessary for all six of them to recover
from the fight and to doctor their many wounds.

Her knuckles were swollen from decking Mikaela and
of course it hadn't helped that she'd punched Darronn
the day prior. Alexi's throat ached and it was still difficult
to talk, but she was far more concerned about her companions and especially Darronn, who had fared far worse
than the others.

His clothing was soaked with blood and claw marks
had slashed his handsome face from his temple, across
one cheek to his lips. His jaw sported a purple bruise,
too, but Alexi had a feeling that was from the blow she'd
landed to his jaw the day before. Darronn made light of
his own injuries, and every time he saw her throat, which
was apparently bruising rapidly, he scowled and muttered a Tarok version of an obscenity under his breath.

While helping the werewolves with their wounded, they had learned that Lord Kir's seer had visioned the attack by Mikaela and her minions. Darronn had thanked the werewolf lord and had promised to one day return the favor.

After helping to burn the carcasses of all the dead, the werewolf pack left, vanishing into the forest as silently as spirits in the mist.

Darronn and Alexi then tended each other's wounds with the Tarok version of a first-aid kit. When they were finished, he took her deeper into the forest and to the Tarok River, away from his brothers, Kira, and Kalina.

The acrid stench of fire and burning flesh faded the farther they went, and was replaced by the rich and welcome scents of the forest. Over one shoulder he carried a saddlebag filled with food and ale. He'd held her hand as they walked, his grip firm and strong. They didn't speak on their way to the river, but the silence between them was charged with both questions and need.

When they reached a secluded location along the river, Darronn dropped the saddlebag and brought Alexi close to him. He cupped her cheeks with his hands, his green eyes studying her as if memorizing all her features. His wood-brown hair fell around his shoulders in a sexy tangled mass, and the gold earring glinted at his ear.

She placed her palms against his muscled chest and clenched his bloodstained tunic in her fists. It still made her heart twist to see the scratches across his face and all his other wounds. He could have died trying to save her.

"Why did you tell me your sister died?" Alexi asked quietly.

Darronn sighed as he stroked her cheek with his thumb. "The sister I knew and loved is dead to me. Once Mikaela betrayed me and my brothers . . . she ceased to exist. In her place is a ruthless, heartless woman." He paused for a moment, then continued, "Because of her treachery I had closed off my heart from loving anyone except my brothers, and then my nephew and niece . . . until I met you."

For a moment Alexi studied Darronn's handsome wounded face. "Why didn't you tell me Alice was alive?"

"Long ago I should have told you of your sister, but I was . . ." He paused as if searching for the right words. His jaw set like he'd made up his mind to be completely honest with her. "I was afraid you would leave me before I had the opportunity to win your heart. Once you told me of your love I intended to explain all to you, but it became more difficult each day. I was afraid you would leave me."

Alexi swallowed the urge to forgive him right away. "You know how important trust is to me."

"I was wrong, firecat," Darronn said, his deep voice causing a familiar tingle in her. He brushed his callused thumb across her cheek and she shivered at the sensual touch. "Will you forgive me?"

"On two conditions," she replied, keeping her tone stern.

Darronn's features remained grave as he nodded and moved one hand to her neck, gently stroking the bruised

189

flesh so lightly she felt nothing but pleasure at the touch. "Anything you name, my love," he murmured, "it is yours."

She clenched her hands tighter in his shirt, ignoring the throb in her knuckles, and gave him a firm, unwavering look. "First, you swear to never withhold anything from me again."

"With all my heart, I pledge that I will always be honest with you," he said, like a Boy Scout swearing a solemn oath, while Alexi barely kept her own expression sober.

"And second," she said, leaning closer to his hard-muscled body, "you must promise to love me as long as we both live."

"My love is forever yours." His mouth curved into a sensual smile and his expressive green eyes flashed with both a fierce kind of joy as well as desire. "Will you . . ." He hesitated, almost like he was afraid of what her answer would be. "I wish for you to become my queen and rule at my side. Will you join with me?"

"I'd be the Queen of Spades?" Alexi grinned at the image of herself decked out like one of the queens on a playing card. "I can't believe I'm actually saying this, Darronn. But I can't imagine being anywhere but with you. Yes, I'll marry—join with you."

Darronn's smile was broad as he moved his hands to her hips. "I love you, firecat."

"About time." Alexi released his shirt and moved her hands up to his neck, beneath his dark wood-brown hair, and pulled him down to meet her. "What are you waiting for? Make love to me already."

Darronn was still smiling when his lips met hers. His mouth was firm and demanding, but loving and caring all at once, and her head spun with a wild kind of desire. She ached for more and a part of her wanted it wild like it was when he released the *tigri* pheromones.

Yet this was incredible . . . seeing and feeling Darronn's gentle side. He was a big fluffy teddy-cat beneath the ferocious exterior.

With a slowness that about drove Alexi out of her mind, Darronn removed her clothing and tossed it aside. When she was naked from head to toe he studied her and gave a primal purr that caused her pussy to ache.

The grass along the riverbank was soft beneath her bare feet. A breeze swept through trees and against her naked skin, caressing her ass, breasts, and pussy, and making her nipples harder than ever. It made her even hotter to be naked when he was fully clothed.

"Have I told you how much you mean to me, firecat?" Darronn cupped both of her breasts in his large palms and rubbed her nipples with his thumbs. "When you left me, I feared that I had lost what means more to me than anything else in this world." His serious green gaze met hers. "Your trust and your love."

Before she could answer he lowered his head and flicked his tongue against one of her nipples. Alexi gasped and closed her eyes, reveling in the sensation of his mouth on her. When he moved to her other nipple, she clenched her hands in his hair and tipped her head back. With the wind blowing against one wet nipple, and his warm mouth fastened to her other, she thought she'd go crazy with need for him.

"Lick me. Please, Master," Alexi said, and his answering groan told her how much he enjoyed her allowing him to control their lovemaking.

"When I choose to reward you, firecat, I will," he murmured in a teasing tone. "Perhaps you need punishment for leaving your Master."

She moaned as he moved his lips to the sensitive place between her breasts. His stubbled cheeks abraded the soft skin as he flicked his tongue along a line down her flat belly to her hairless mound. "I want your thighs spread wider," he said in that commanding tone she loved.

"Yes, Master." Alexi needed to come so badly that her knees were weak. Bracing her hands on his shoulders, she moved her legs farther apart, granting him full access to her wet folds.

Darronn continued his sensual punishment, rubbing his stubble-roughened cheeks and his nose over her mound and between her thighs. "Your taste, your scent," he murmured as he spread her folds with his fingers, "I can never get enough." And then he licked her in one long swipe of his rough tongue.

Alexi gasped and tightened her hold on his shoulders. Her legs trembled, she was so close to coming. But he was a master tease, driving his tongue into her core one moment, then flicking her clit with his rough tongue the next.

Darronn slid two fingers inside her and began to thrust while he sucked her clit. Heat swept over Alexi and she cried out as her orgasm flamed through her. All of the emotion she'd experienced in the last two days added fuel to the intensity of her climax until it was all burned away and what was left was simply her love for her man.

She was still riding her orgasm when Darronn got to his feet and caught her by the shoulders and gave her a fierce kiss. She tasted herself on his tongue and lips, caught her scent mingling with his elemental male musk. He released her and started to pull off his tunic, but Alexi stopped him by putting her hand on his.

"Take me now," she said, "with your clothes on."

He growled and picked her up, then laid her in a soft patch of grass. The ever-present roar of the river joined with the blood rushing in her ears as he unfastened his leather pants, released his powerful erection, and lowered himself between her thighs. He placed his cock to the entrance of her core, then hooked his arms beneath her knees and spread her farther open.

He was so gorgeous, so fierce looking as he stared down at her. Sweat trickled down his injured cheek and he tensed his jaw. "I claim you, firecat."

"No," she said. "I claim *you*. You're mine, Darronn."

With a shout of triumph, Darronn thrust his cock inside her. Alexi's already sensitive folds spasmed and she arched up to meet him, taking him deep. His leather-clad hips chafed her inner thighs and brushed her folds, making the moment all the more exciting. She loved the way his black clothing looked against her pale skin as she watched his cock moving in and out of her.

Another orgasm built up inside Alexi, and this time her cry was loud and strong when she came. Darronn continued to fuck her, not letting up until she came two more times. He roared when he came and she felt the powerful throb of his cock inside her, felt the warmth of his semen filling her.

Darronn lowered her legs and released his hold on her thighs, then pressed close without putting all his weight on Alexi. Her core still contracted around his cock in small bursts, and she wondered if she'd ever stop coming.

"I love you, firecat," he murmured as he brushed his lips over hers. "Forever."

The following day's journey across the Singing Plains lasted forever as far as Alexi was concerned. Tok and the other *jul* didn't seem to mind the pace she kept, and Darronn had expressed his amusement at her single-mindedness. She'd even managed to ignore his sensual teasing when he'd ridden behind her on Tok's back.

Before the trip started that morning, Alexi had also come to an understanding with both Karn and Ty—they didn't try to boss her around, and she didn't kick them in the nuts.

Her future husband alternated between riding behind her on *jul*-back, and loping alongside as a tiger. He was beautiful no matter what form he took, and her heart and soul filled with a sense of sheer happiness that she'd never experienced before.

Of course the elation she felt at the thought of seeing her sister again made her want to jump off the horse-beast and sprint ahead.

Damn it. I'd probably get there faster if I did run, she grumbled in her thoughts.

After following the Tarok River for miles and miles and miles across the grassy plains, they reached a jungle. And after hours of traveling through palm trees and vines, they finally reached the Kingdom of Hearts.

Alexi was sure she would bounce right off Tok, she was so excited. "Do you think she knows we're coming?" she asked Darronn, who was again riding behind her on the *jul*.

"We did not send a messenger," Darronn said as they emerged from out of the dim jungle into a sunlit clearing. "Unless one of Jarronn's sorcerers foretold our arrival, it is likely they are not expecting us."

He kissed the bruised skin at the back of her neck as they stopped at a waterfall and a set of tiered pools, several yards from the turreted castle. In an easy movement he dismounted and helped Alexi down. Her legs felt bowlegged after all the riding, her butt was sore, her neck ached, and her knuckles were swollen, but right now she couldn't be happier. She was going to see Alice . . . and she was in love with Darronn.

Kalina and Kira were still dismounting when Alexi started to head toward the castle. She knew it was the back entrance, but it was magnificent, the white walls rising up into the sky and sparkling in the late afternoon sunshine.

"Wait, firecat." Darronn caught up to her and grasped her arm, bringing her to a halt.

"I can't." Alexi was so anxious and jittery to see her sister she felt wired, like she'd had a whole pot of Starbucks French Roast. *"Hurry."*

"Your sister has changed," he said as she met his serious green eyes. "Know that she is happy."

Alexi frowned. "What—" But she stopped as she heard the sound of a woman's laughter and giggles of small children.

Her gaze cut toward the castle and her jaw dropped at the sight of a beautiful naked woman with long white-blond hair. A collar of diamonds with hearts made of rubies circled her neck and a ruby and diamond chain swung from one nipple to the other.

The woman wore nothing else but a radiant smile as she trailed behind a pair of toddlers. Her blue-green eyes sparkled as she said, "Lance and Lexi, go say hello to your uncles."

The toddlers suddenly morphed into tiger cubs and bounded across the grass toward the men in Alexi's group. Karn and Ty both grinned as they each gathered a cub into his arms.

"Oh. My. God," Alexi whispered.

Alice. The naked woman was her sister.

"It's great to see you all," Alice said as her gaze quickly traveled the group. "We didn't expect—" Her gaze rested on Alexi and her eyes widened. "Alexi?" she whispered.

Naked or not, Alexi was so happy to see her sister that she launched herself at Alice, wrapped her arms around her, and squeezed her tight. "We thought you were dead. Well, I didn't but everyone else did, and I never stopped looking for you." Alexi's words came out in a rush, her tears flowing, as she held her sister tight. "A couple of days ago I found out you were here and I couldn't believe it. I still can't believe it."

Alice was sobbing, too. "God, I've missed you so much."

For a long time they held each other tight. Alexi didn't want to let Alice go, afraid it would all be a dream and her sister would disappear again.

When they finally pulled away, Alexi saw that her companions had slipped away with the tiger cubs, apparently giving the sisters time to themselves.

Alexi shook her head. "You look so *different.* You've always been beautiful, but now, you're absolutely gorgeous."

Instead of denying it as she always had when complimented in the past, Alice simply smiled and said, "Thank you."

"And you're naked."

"Like you haven't seen me naked before." Alice gave

her a mischievous grin. "As kids when we were growing up, in the locker room, when we went skinny-dipping— lots of times."

Alexi rolled her eyes. "Oh, like this isn't *totally* different."

Her twin grinned, but then her gaze rested on Alexi's throat. Alice's expression turned horrified as she reached up with her fingers and lightly touched the bruised area. "What happened? Who did this? I'll have them executed or something."

Alexi almost laughed as she imagined the Queen of Hearts crying out *"Off with her head!"* But the look on her sister's face kept her sober. Although if Alice offered her some strawberry tarts, Alexi knew she'd giggle for sure—and she wasn't the giggly type.

"I'm all right. Really." Alexi shrugged, not wanting to make this moment serious. "Yesterday Darronn saved my life from some witch named Mikaela."

Alice dropped her hand and straightened. Her aqua eyes flashed an incredible fury that Alexi had never witnessed in her sister before. "Ooooh, that *bitch*. It was bad enough she went after me, but you? *I'll* kill her."

"Not likely," a deep masculine voice said from behind them. "I would never let Mikaela near you."

"Yes, Milord," Alice murmured, her expression changing to one of pleasure as she lowered her eyes.

Alexi's gaze cut to the gorgeous man with brilliant green eyes, hair black as nightfall, and a light beard. A heart tattoo crossed his biceps and she realized at once this was Darronn's brother Jarronn, the King of Hearts.

He studied her as though expecting her to lower her eyes like Alice had. Instead Alexi tilted her head back and glared at him. "What have you done to my sister? How dare you treat her as though she's subservient to you?"

"May I speak, Milord?" Alice asked before Jarronn could respond.

"Of course, love," he murmured as he put his fingers under Alice's chin and raised it so that their eyes met. He brushed his lips across hers and she smiled . . . a sort of melty-totally-in-love smile.

Alexi gritted her teeth and clenched her fists at her sides. She couldn't believe that Alice allowed him to treat her this way.

But Alice's smile was luminous as she turned to Alexi. "I love everything about my life here, Lex. I like being dominated by Jarronn. I wouldn't put up with it from anyone else. But with him, it turns me on and it feels right."

"Did he drug you or use that *tigri* stuff on you to make you feel this way?" Alexi asked, ready to deck Jarronn. "I don't care if he's considered a god here, he'll regret it if he did."

"It's probably a good thing you don't have your can of Mace." Alice laughed and darted a sensual look at Jarronn. "Although I've seen you smash a few nuts on occasion."

"So I have heard," Jarronn said, the corner of his mouth quirking. "Darronn and Ty gave me fair warning to guard my bollocks before I joined you."

Alice burst out laughing and said, "You didn't!" then clapped her hand over her mouth.

Alexi nodded and cast Jarronn a look meant to let him know how serious she was when she told him, "And if I find out this guy has done anything to you that you didn't want, then he certainly won't be having any more kids."

Jarronn winced and Alice snickered behind her hand. The king gave her a commanding yet sensual and utterly adoring look as he murmured, "Is punishment in order, wench?"

Alice bit her lower lip and her nipples grew so hard that Alexi swore she saw the diamond and ruby chain levitate between them. "If it pleases you, Milord."

The king reached up and tweaked one of Alice's nipples. "That it will."

Amazed that her sister obviously got off on all this, Alexi shook her head. "It's a damn good thing Alice is happy," Alexi muttered. "A damn good thing."

CHAPTER FOURTEEN

A TAROK WEEK AFTER THEIR ARRIVAL IN Hearts, Darronn and Alexi returned to Spades to be joined as king and queen. Not only did Karn, Ty, Kira, and Kalina accompany them back, but so did Alice, Jarronn, Lexi, and Lance, along with a small army of warriors who escorted them.

As Alexi prepared for the joining ceremony, she couldn't get over the fact that Lexi and Lance were only six Tarok months old. They seemed so much older. In Earth time, the children would probably not even be walking yet. Being werecubs, though, they were growing so much faster than if they were fully human.

Home. Alexi ran a brush through her auburn hair as her thoughts turned toward the Kingdom of Spades and her husband-to-be. *It really* does *feel like home here in Spades.* She wasn't sure she'd ever get used to the lack of "modern conveniences," but the magic people had here made up for most of what Alexi would miss.

By her own request, she was alone in the king and queen's chambers preparing for the ceremony. She'd promised Alice and Kalina that she would call for them soon, but she needed a few moments to herself.

I can't believe I'm getting married.

And Alexi certainly was having a hard time getting used to the idea that one day she would become part of the weretiger family. Every time they made love and Darronn released his *tigri* pheromones, she was coming closer and closer to becoming a weretigress. The thought more than excited her. How cool it would be to shape-shift like Darronn, and to live for centuries.

After setting the gold-handled brush on the dressing table, Alexi moved before the full-length mirror and studied her reflection. Thoughts of the "wedding" whirled in her mind. She'd never truly believed she would get married. Never thought she would ever meet a man like Darronn. Yet she had.

And he's all mine.

Yeah, she'd have to agree that she was getting everything wonderful *in spades.*

Smiling at her image, Alexi let her gaze travel over the beautiful outfit Darronn had had specially made for her to wear for their joining day. With a few modifications, he'd had the seamstress pattern it after the clothing she had worn when he brought her through the looking glass. She brought her fingers to the sparkly gold midriff top and lightly touched the fringe made of black diamonds and gold beads. The fringe was absolutely stunning and probably worth more than all her assets combined back in San Francisco.

At the thought of her home, she couldn't help but wish Annie and Awai could be here for her joining day. She shook her head at her reflection as she remembered what she had said to Annie in the bar, *"It's nice to have someone looking after me for a change."* It certainly did feel good having Darronn to watch over her.

Alexi turned slightly so that she could see her image from the side. Instead of cap sleeves, the top had billowy sleeves that were slit along each side, revealing her slender arms. The front of the blouse just covered her breasts and was fastened beneath them with a spade made from a black diamond. Her flat belly was exposed and her gold tiger charm glittered at her navel. The miniskirt was made of the same fabric as the top, and barely covered her ass and her mound. She didn't have any underwear on, since no one in this world seemed to even know what bras and panties were. Jeez, if she dared to bend over, anyone looking would get one hell of a view.

Not that half the village hadn't witnessed her Lady Godiva ride the day she arrived in Spades.

She had to grin at the memory of how Darronn's attempt at "training" her had backfired on him.

The bruise around her neck had faded quickly, thanks to one of the healers in Hearts, and her voice was no longer hoarse from being almost strangled to death. The healers had also treated the claw marks on Darronn's face, but scars now crossed his stubbled cheek.

Apparently they could do nothing for the scars because the wound had been so deep, but Alexi thought they only made him even more dangerously handsome.

Alexi's gaze moved from her throat, down her image's length, then rested on her high heels. Somehow the magicians here had taken her lipstick-red stilettos and had made them into the same beautiful gold as her blouse and skirt and then had put black diamond spades at the fastening. After that first time together with Darronn, her thigh-high nylons had been put away until now. He loved the way the line ran up the back of her leg, and she couldn't wait for him to see the accessory she'd added to her wedding wardrobe.

All the gold she was wearing went well with her auburn hair, which flowed long and loose about her shoulders, and the gold bracelets she wore at either wrist. Alexi smiled. Maybe afterward Darronn would fasten her wrists together and then tie her up.

The week that Alexi spent with her sister in Hearts had sped by so quickly that she felt as if she'd just arrived. She loved her niece and nephew, and when she was around them she often felt something stir inside her, as though she might enjoy having children of her own, too.

Damn biological clock, anyway.

At first it had been hard getting used to her sister being so submissive around Jarronn. But after a while, Alexi had realized that Alice and Jarronn's relationship was truly on equal footing and that both enjoyed their roles. Alice held power over his pleasure and making him happy, which perhaps made her in some ways more powerful than her husband.

What pleased Alexi most was that her twin finally was completely comfortable in her own skin. Thanks to Jarronn, Alice now loved herself for who she was.

Alexi smiled. It was wonderful to see her sister so happy.

The one thing Alexi *really* hadn't been thrilled about was when she had learned about the mind-bond thing where Alice had been taken by all four brothers at once. Knowing that Darronn had participated had really bothered Alexi at first. But once she understood the reason behind it, and that the mind-bond had saved Alice's life, Alexi was able to let it go. It was a one-time deal, and it had happened before she ever met Darronn, so she could live with that.

Alexi heard a light knock on the door, and her heart began to pound. It was time.

She tossed her hair over her shoulder and smiled.

Bring it on.

With a large gathering of villagers and weretigers and weretigresses, Darronn paced the meadow where he had first captured his future queen. If Alexi's carriage did not arrive soon, he would surely wear a trench through the grass.

Much effort and planning had gone into the day. Darronn had scouts mounted far and wide to detect

Mikaela and her *bakir* should they attempt to invade his realm. His legion of warriors were ever at the ready.

A crisp spring morning breeze invigorated him while thoughts of his woman caused his cock to stir beneath his leather breeches. Smells of sun-warmed grass mingled with the perfume of starflowers and pine. Laughter and conversation filled the air along with feelings of promise, of renewal, and hope.

Although Alexi had once said she never intended to have children, Darronn wanted children of his own with his bride, but he would not force her. He would be happy to have her as his queen forevermore.

His gaze rested on the beautiful Queen of Hearts, who appeared quite anxious without her cubs at her side. She had been reluctant to leave them with the nanny and far from her sight, but Jarronn had reminded her that a binding ceremony was no place for children, and Alice had quickly agreed.

The binding ceremony. In keeping with his promise to remain truthful, Darronn had explained the traditional ceremony to Alexi even though he had known she would not approve. She had reacted as he thought she would, her aqua eyes blazing fury and threatening to unman him if he dared such a thing. He had quickly reassured her that he had no desire to share his future queen in any way, including baring her flesh or taking her before a crowd.

Today he would break with tradition, and damn the consequences.

The clatter of hooves and carriage met Darronn's

sensitive hearing, and he cut his gaze in the direction of the noise. For an eternity he waited, then the gilded carriage came into view, drawn by three golden *jul* steeds. Voices lowered until a hush covered the land, broken only by the sound of the approaching carriage bearing his mate within. Finally it came to an abrupt stop behind the seated crowd.

Darronn's heart nearly thumped through his chest while he waited. Ty approached the carriage and opened the door, and Darronn almost smiled at the thought of his brother taking care to guard his bollocks as he assisted the future Queen of Spades.

But as the door opened and Alexi emerged from the carriage, the crowd gasped in unison and Darronn's heart ceased to beat. She was more than breathtaking in the golden adornments. Ty helped her step from the carriage then escorted her to the black velvet carpeting that stretched from the coach to Darronn's feet. Ty bowed and moved away.

Black diamonds glittered and flashed as Alexi walked toward Darronn. Her smile was radiant and confident, her chin held high. Her nipples peaked under the thin gold material and in the sunshine he swore he saw them through the fabric. Waiting for his touch, for his mouth. The lower portion of her clothing barely covered her mons, and dear skies above, she was wearing the black stockings on her legs that nearly drove him mad with desire when he first saw her.

Now he was near to spilling his seed in his breeches, crowd or no.

When Alexi reached him he took both her hands in his and smiled at his mate.

And then he lowered himself to one knee, worshiping his future queen.

Murmurs rolled through the crowd and Alexi's eyes widened with obvious surprise.

"My love," Darronn said, his voice carrying across the meadow. Every other voice went still. "I will love and cherish you all my days upon this world. Will you take me as your mate, your king, and your equal?"

Alexi's gaze filled with wonder as she looked down at him and smiled. In the very next moment she knelt with him and the crowd gave a collective sigh. Darronn's heart swelled as his woman chose to join him, to show their unity as king and queen.

"Darronn," Alexi said, her voice clear as she spoke, "I love you more each and every day. I will take you as my mate, my king, my equal . . . and as the father of our future children."

Alexi's declaration in front of his family and his subjects almost shocked him speechless. She had agreed to all that he asked of her—and to bear his children.

Darronn ignored the buzz from the crowd as he held his hand out, hopeful that Alexi would choose to accept what he offered. "My gift to you. Not a sign of ownership, but a symbol of my love."

A smile lifted the corners of her mouth as she ran her fingertip over the white diamond collar that had spades along it made with black diamonds. "It is beautiful, Darronn. I accept your gift."

Relief and joy filled his heart and soul. Carefully he fastened the collar around her elegant neck. It glittered in the morning sunlight, almost as brilliant as Alexi's smile.

Gripping her shoulders tight, Darronn lowered his mouth to hers and kissed her softly, tenderly. He slipped his tongue between her lips, and she took him in, drawing him deeper and deeper.

Darronn slid one hand into her silken auburn hair, cupping the back of her head while his other hand moved to her ass and he pressed her closer, tighter, ensuring she would feel his erection against her belly. He clenched his hand in the soft golden material of her skirt, drawing it up above her buttocks, when he heard the sound of voices.

Damnation. For that beautiful moment he had forgotten they were not alone.

With a groan he pulled away from her, but for a long moment he could only gaze at her. "I love you, firecat."

The look on Darronn's handsome, scarred face made Alexi feel like a teenager with a crush on a rock star. Loopy and silly and infatuated and in love. And in lust, definitely major lust.

"Let's get out of here," she said, bringing her fingers to the collar at her throat and gently stroking it. "Now."

That feral gleam returned to his eyes as he helped her stand. In the next moment Alexi shrieked as he grabbed her around the waist with one arm, flung her over his shoulder, and headed down the black velvet carpeting.

Laughter and applause followed them and Alexi grinned. Darronn was asserting his dominance over her sexually, and she loved it. Blood rushed to her head as he strode toward the gilded enclosed carriage, but she had her wits about her enough to realize there was a massive orgy going on behind them. Darronn had explained to her how the weretiger ceremony usually worked, and it always ended in a bout of free love, not unlike San Francisco in the sixties.

She did see Jarronn carrying Alice off into the woods. From what Alice had told Alexi, once all that bonding stuff was over, the High King wasn't about to share his Queen in any fashion.

When they reached the carriage, Darronn settled her inside on the plush black velvet seat that was wide enough to be a twin bed. He climbed in after her and shut the door. Morning light poured in through the sunroof and Alexi could clearly see the love and lust in her new husband's eyes.

The carriage started moving and the small bouncing motions caused jolts to shoot through her pussy. Damn but she was hot for Darronn.

"You have made me a king among men this day," he murmured as he knelt before her and gently pushed her so that she reclined against the black velvet cushions.

"What do you intend to do to your queen?" Alexi shifted so that her tiny gold skirt slid up a bit, almost showing her mound.

"Reward her." Darronn purred as he grasped her knees and moved between her thighs. Her skirt hiked up to her hips and she was totally exposed to his gaze. His purr turned into an untamed growl as he moved his face to her mound and sniffed, scenting her.

The mere action made Alexi's clit twitch and she raised her hips. "Lick me. *Now.*"

"Such impudence." He slid his fingers along the outside of her stocking-clad thighs, to the flesh above. His hands pushed her skirt all the way to her waist, the spade tattoo at his wrist dark against her pale skin. "Perhaps it is punishment you require . . . or desire," he murmured.

The sensual assurance in his voice set her on fire. "Well, you certainly can't tie me up in here."

"My little wench must learn to curb her tongue." Darronn caught both her wrists and raised them over her head.

She glanced at the carriage's ceiling and saw a loop positioned above her, yet a little back. *Spoke too soon.* A thrill shot through her belly straight to between her thighs.

His movements were quick and sure as he produced a leather strap from thin air, magically fastened her wrists together with her bracelets, and tied her to the loop above.

How did he *do* that—tie her up so fast she barely had time to catch her breath?

"Arch your back, wench," he ordered, his eyes focused on her breasts.

Alexi's nipples grew even harder beneath his gaze as she pulled against her bonds. "Make me."

Darronn growled and placed his hand to the black

diamond pin. It slipped off, releasing its hold on the material, which fell away from her breasts.

It felt wonderfully wanton to have her body bared to his gaze while she was bound. And wearing the diamond collar made her even more excited.

He lowered his head and his warm breath brushed her nipples. Instinctively she arched toward his mouth and too late realized she had done exactly as he'd commanded her to.

Triumph flashed in his eyes.

"Suck my nipples," she demanded, arching toward him even more.

Ignoring her, he nuzzled first one, and then the other. "How must you ask, wench?"

Darronn was going to drive her out of her mind if she didn't give in—not to mention she really got off when he mastered her sexually. "Please suck my nipples, my King," she said, trying to keep her tone as contrite as possible.

"Mayhap." He trailed his lips along the flesh between her breasts and her belly, down to her navel where he flicked his tongue over her tiger charm.

Alexi couldn't help the moan that escaped at his sensual torture. She pulled against her bonds and widened her thighs. "I need you, Master."

A rumbling purr rose up within him and he rewarded her by moving his mouth to one of her nipples. She thrashed against her bonds as he licked and sucked it, and cried out at the sheer pleasure when he treated her other nipple with the same regard.

When he abandoned her breasts and moved lower, she almost sobbed with her need to come. "Please lick my clit, Master."

"Only if you promise you will not climax without my permission." He laved the inside of her thigh with his rough tongue. "Do you understand, wench?"

She raised her hips up, offering herself to him. "Yes, my King."

Darronn slid his hands beneath her ass and began licking and sucking at her clit and her folds. "Damn," she muttered, "I'm so close, Darronn." But he moved to another area, keeping her from coming and not giving her permission.

He paused and looked up at her. Was there anything sexier than seeing Darronn's face between her thighs?

Yeah. Watching his cock slide in and out.

"May I come, Master?" she asked as he resumed driving her out of her mind.

"No," he said, then zeroed in on her clit.

"I—I have to come, Master. Fuck me, please!"

Darronn gave one long suck of her clit and Alexi's orgasm exploded through her. Every jolt of the carriage, every flick of Darronn's tongue, drove her climax on and on until she was sure it was possible to die from an orgasm overdose.

When he finally let up, Darronn stood and released her bonds, yet kept her wrists fastened at her bracelets. "You have earned a punishment, wench," he said.

Alexi was still trembling from aftershocks and couldn't speak as he turned her around so that her back was to him and she was kneeling on the wide seat. In a few quick movements, he had her bound to a different loop, this one in front of her. Darronn forced her to stretch forward, not allowing her to move her knees. As her weight pulled against her bonds, the fringe along her blouse dangled against her sensitive nipples, turning her on even more.

Behind her Darronn pushed her skirt back up over her hips, exposing her ass. "Do you understand your punishment?" he asked.

"Yes, Master," Alexi said, hoping he used that black strap of his to swat her. "For coming when I'm not supposed to."

She heard the sound of cloth being undone, then the tip of his erection was suddenly at the entrance to her core. In the next moment she felt the flat of his hand and heard the slap of his palm against her flesh as he smacked her ass while at the same time he drove his cock into her.

Alexi screamed with the incredible pleasure that flooded through her. Outside the carriage the whinny of one of the *jul* mingled with the clip-clop of hooves and carriage wheels rumbling over the road.

With every thrust of Darronn's cock, and every swat of his hand, and every jolt of the carriage, Alexi flew higher and higher. "Yeah. Fuck me, Your Highness," she said. "Fuck me harder."

"Your ass is a lovely shade of rose," he murmured as he obliged, driving in and out with more force. "And your core . . . it grips my cock like the finest of gloves."

Fireworks burst in Alexi's mind and her climax roared through her. Darronn kept thrusting, drawing out her orgasm as he continued to slap her ass.

A tremendous roar filled the carriage as he reached his peak and his semen filled her core.

"My firecat." He slumped against her, his cock still in her, his warm body pressed tight to hers. "I love you."

When they reached the château, and had arranged their clothing, Darronn carried Alexi in his arms, straight to their bedroom, and then closed the door behind them. She was still light-headed from the countless orgasms in the carriage and a little disoriented when he set her on her feet.

But she sobered up immediately when she saw the mirror, the magical looking glass, standing in the corner of their chambers.

Almost in a trance she moved toward it. She stepped onto the black velvet rug at the foot of the mirror, then placed her palm flat against its cool surface and studied her unkempt, well-fucked appearance. The diamond collar glittered and sparkled with every movement she made.

"The looking glass is my other binding gift to you." Darronn moved behind her and wrapped his arms around her waist and she saw how good they looked together. "Kalina will teach you how to use it before she leaves with Karn for the Kingdom of Diamonds."

"Wow." She moved her hand to the elaborate frame and stroked it. "This is incredible, Darronn."

He turned her a bit as he moved around her so that they were facing each other, their sides to the mirror. "You are incredible, my love."

She raised her hand and trailed it across the scars on his cheek. "You are an amazing man."

Gently Darronn kissed Alexi. Her mind spun and she was barely conscious of him lowering her to the black rug at their feet. With motions so smooth it had to be magic, her blouse fell away from her breasts, her skirt was up around her waist, and Darronn's cock was freed from his breeches. He raised up her legs so that her stocking-clad ankles were up around his neck, her gold stilettos still on her feet.

"Watch me take you in the looking glass," he said, his voice rumbling with desire.

She followed his gaze to the mirror and her belly twisted at the sight of his cock ready to drive into her. His eyes met hers in the reflection, and then he plunged inside her core.

Alexi gasped from the sensation of him thrusting inside her, and from what it looked like to watch Darronn making love to her. The diamond collar seemed to sparkle even more as he drove his cock in and out of her.

Her orgasm completely shattered her this time. Fast and sudden, it fractured her very being, and it was a wonder the looking glass didn't crack from the sound of her scream.

Darronn's roar followed her cry and his cock pulsated inside her as he came.

Once the last of their orgasms ebbed, he rolled off

her to her side. He arranged them so that they were both staring into the mirror, her back to him.

Propping himself on one elbow, he smiled as their gazes met in the looking glass.

Alexi returned his smile. "I'm so happy you brought me into your world, Darronn."

"I would have none other," he murmured as he kissed her neck, "for you are my Queen of Spades."

EPILOGUE

PERSISTENT KNOCKING AT THE FRONT DOOR jarred Annie Travis from her artistic trance. She blinked the fog from her mind, slowly returning to reality. A glance to the window told her that from the time she'd started working on her painting hours had fled by rather than minutes. The sun now hung low over the ocean, its golden ripples leading from the glowing orb across the water to the shore. A spectacular sunset of oranges, blues, and pinks streaked the horizon.

More knocks, and Annie frowned as she eyed the door. Should she answer, or hope whoever it was went away?

"Annie! I know you're in there!" came Aunt Awai's no-nonsense voice through the door. "Stop moping and open up."

"I'm not moping," Annie grumbled under her breath as she tossed her brush onto her palette, stood, and stretched her cramped muscles. The movement caused cool air to rush over her nipples and they stood out hard and tight. Heat flushed over Annie as she realized she was still naked from the waist up. She quickly grabbed her T-shirt and yanked it over her head.

"Annie!" Awai's tone notched up to her *I'm-gonna-huff-and-puff-and-blow-your-house-down* voice.

"Coming," Annie shouted. She pushed her glasses up her nose, threw her braid over her shoulder, and padded across the worn carpet to the door. Abra watched from her perch on the back of the couch. The cat had her little chin up high, doing her best to show she was queen of Annie's realm.

"What, are you naked or something?" Awai said from outside, and Annie's cheeks heated even more. "Open the damn door already."

"Yeah, yeah." When Annie reached the door she wiped her sweating palms on her black jeans. She didn't bother to look through the peephole—no doubt at all that it was her aunt, the human whirlwind. She unlatched the chain lock, then opened the door.

As always, Awai was sheer elegance with her black hair in a neat chignon at her nape and wearing one of her usual designer outfits. This one had a black skirt and matching mandarin-collared jacket, her blouse a splash of amethyst in a vivid but gorgeous contrast.

Her aunt was holding two paper bags, one in each arm. "Took you long enough," she said before Annie had a chance to greet her.

Awai bustled through the doorway and Annie was

looking out into late afternoon sunshine instead of her aunt. "Uh, hello?"

The warm smell of fresh-baked bread and something spicy followed Awai as she headed straight into the apartment's kitchenette. Annie's stomach growled.

"I heard that," Awai said as she plopped the bags onto the counter. Without pause, she went to the oven, and turned it on. "I knew you'd be painting and moping."

"I wasn't moping." Annie shut the front door and followed her aunt into the tiny kitchen, the linoleum cool to her bare feet. "What in heaven's name are you doing?"

"Making us dinner." Awai smiled as her dark eyes met Annie's. "I figured you'd be in need of more than just Abra for company this evening."

Annie raised an eyebrow. "Auntie, you don't cook."

"Ah, but I make one hell of a mean warmed-up lasagna." Awai reached for one of the shopping bags and pulled out a loaf of French bread, a packaged salad, a bottle of Annie's favorite brand of merlot, and an aluminum pan with MAMMA MIA'S ITALIAN GRILL stamped across the cardboard top.

"Mmmmm. My favorite." Annie peeked in the other bag. "Oooh, and you brought spumoni, too. I'll put it in the freezer."

Annie had to admit it was fun chatting with her dynamo aunt, and it helped to not be alone while she was thinking about her missing cousins. Awai was actually their aunt by marriage, not blood, and she only had four years on Annie, who had just passed her thirtieth birthday.

Awai's being there to help her through this tough day reminded Annie of that night a year ago when she'd taken Alexi out for drinks and dinner to help get her mind off Alice.

The night she up and disappeared. Some idea that was, getting her drunk.

It wasn't long before dinner was served and Annie and Awai were sitting at the small oak table in the kitchen nook and Abra was rubbing her head against Annie's feet beneath the table. Awai chatted about the latest account she'd won over to her advertising firm, and of the gorgeous blond man she'd just met at the club last night.

"Which club?" Annie asked before taking a sip of her merlot.

As her eyes met Annie's, Awai gave a small shrug. "A BDSM club."

Annie choked on her wine and it shot up her nose. She grabbed her napkin and managed to cover her mouth before she spewed merlot everywhere.

"Are you all right, sweets?" Awai asked as if she'd just said she'd found toilet paper on sale at the grocery store instead of announcing she'd gone to a BDSM club.

When she'd sufficiently recovered, Annie patted her mouth with the napkin then set it on her empty plate. "That's why you were wearing that tight leather dress and those thigh-high boots when I came by to ask you to go with me to Alexi's last year. You weren't off to a masquerade party. You were going to a BDSM club."

Awai smiled and raised her glass. "Does it bother you that I'm a Dominatrix? That's Domme for short."

Annie almost choked again as she visualized her aunt wearing that same outfit and whipping a submissive male. "Um, no. Not at all."

Cocking her head to one side, Awai said, "You should come with me sometime and find a good Dom. You're a born submissive, you know."

"I don't think so." Annie shook her head. "I'm not into, ah, whips and handcuffs."

Awai pushed aside her plate and folded her arms on the table as she gave Annie that penetrating look of hers that was sure to have won over plenty of accounts . . . and probably submissives, too. "Annie, for a sub, giving up control is more than bondage, more than pleasure and pain. It's power. You have total control over your Master's pleasure. You hold all the cards."

Meeting her aunt's gaze head-on, Annie asked, "Why are you a Domme?"

With a shrug Awai leaned back in her chair. "I enjoy having men obeying my every whim."

"Like they do at the agency?" Annie asked as she arched one eyebrow.

The corner of Awai's mouth curved. "Something like that."

Annie pulled her braid over her shoulder and absently played with the end of it. "If the submissive has all the control, then why aren't you a sub?"

For a moment Awai was silent. When she finally spoke she said, "Until I truly learned the concept behind

BDSM, I always thought the Domme had the power." She brushed imaginary lint off her black skirt. "And now, I enjoy being a Domme." But something in Awai's eyes held just a tinge of regret.

Before Annie could say anything, Awai was up and out of her chair, heading toward the easel in the living room. "So, what are you working on? Something depressing, right?"

Annie rolled her eyes, but then she realized she had no idea what she'd done during those hours of painting today. With Abra at her heels, Annie followed her aunt to the easel.

Awai folded her arms and pursed her lips. "Oh, definitely morbid, but I like it."

Annie's frown deepened but when she reached the easel and stopped in front of the canvas, her eyes widened.

Cocking one eyebrow, Awai cut Annie a questioning glance. "Looks like it came right out of *Wuthering Heights*."

"Yeah, it does." Annie's practiced eye scanned her work. It wasn't quite finished, but it was damn good, if not murky and mysterious. Maybe it was a sign that she was more down about her cousins' disappearances than she'd thought.

A sprawling but gloomy mansion stood dark and foreboding in the background with only a single window dimly lit from within, as if by candlelight. Lightning illuminated the scene just enough that the viewer could see skeleton trees bowing close to the ground from raging winds, and in the distance one could see the white-caps upon a body of water below sheer black cliffs. In the lower right-hand corner was a single magnolia bloom lying in the grass, its petals pure cream beside a shadow.

She narrowed her gaze. A man's shadow. How odd.

"Well, this is interesting," Awai said, breaking into Annie's thoughts. "How did you come up with it?"

Annie shook her head. "I have no idea. The twins are still missing . . . maybe it's bothering me even more than I thought."

Awai stayed for a while longer, long enough to share the spumoni and to polish off the bottle of wine. Annie wasn't much of a drinker usually, and tonight she'd had two glasses of merlot. She felt mellow and relaxed, and definitely ready for bed.

Once Awai had left in a cab for her San Francisco apartment, Annie went back to the painting. After she moved the easel in front of her overstuffed armchair, she sat and studied her day's work, her elbow resting on her knee, her chin in her hand. Her braid fell over her opposite shoulder as she tried to interpret her own work. Abra jumped onto the armrest and started batting the end of Annie's braid.

Where the heck did I get this from?

The picture had a brooding, gothic feel to it. It was unlike her usual landscapes and seascapes, but was still in her distinctive style. The painting was fascinating, really. She rarely had dwellings in her work, and this mausoleum of a mansion was beyond anything she thought herself capable of. Perhaps it was so captivating because it reminded her of the gothic romance novels her grandmother was always reading when Annie was young and still lived in Tennessee.

Stifling a yawn, Annie rose and turned away from the painting when she heard the crack of thunder. Abra hissed and arched her back then darted under the end table. Lights in her apartment flickered.

Everything went completely dark.

Annie frowned. They never had thunderstorms in the Bay Area because of the cool onshore flow of air from the Pacific. She started to go to the window when a flash lit up her dark apartment for a moment. Thunder boomed again, rattling her windows.

But the lightning flash hadn't come from outside.

It had come from her painting.

A strange buzzing started in Annie's ears as she moved back toward the painting—and her heart started pounding like mad.

She saw the same scene she had painted, only now it looked like a very tall and narrow television screen rather than a canvas. It was raining in the picture and trees swayed in fierce gusts of wind. She could even hear the haunting sound of wind blowing and could feel wet air gusting from the painting. It rushed across her face and misted her glasses. She saw something that looked like a very large cat stalking across the picture . . . a white tiger.

Abra hissed again from her hiding place, this time louder and much more fierce.

Goose bumps prickled Annie's skin and her nipples pebbled beneath her T-shirt.

"Too much wine, sugar," she murmured as she pulled off her glasses that were now too fogged to see through. "This is why you don't normally drink."

Although hallucinating after only having two goblets of wine was mighty strange.

Lightning flashed in the picture again and Annie jumped. In the brief illumination she saw the magnolia bloom—only this time a man was holding it.

A man. In the picture. Looking directly at her.

He moved closer, so that he filled the scene, and she could hardly see anything around him. Wind tugged at his black hair and clothing, which were soaked from the rain. He was dressed in an equally black shirt and pants, but he was too close for her to be able to see what he wore on his feet. His eyes were black, too. Dark and haunting.

The man held his free hand out to her, and she took an automatic step back.

"Come, Annie," he said in a deep, husky voice that caused a thrill to zip through her belly. "It is time."

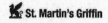